GILBERT MORRIS

THE FAR
FIELDS
SERIES #2

THE REMNANT

Book 2 of 1
Beyond The River

STARBURST PUBLISHERS

P. O. Box 4123, Lancaster, Pennsylvania 17604

To schedule Author appearances write:
Author Appearances, Starburst Promotions, P.O. Box 4123,
Lancaster, Pennsylvania 17604 or call (717) 293-0939

Credits:
Cover art by Kerne Erickson

THE REMNANT

First Printing, August 1997

ISBN: 0-914984-918
Library of Congress Catalog Number 96-072369
Printed in the United States of America

Table of Contents

One	**Escape From Haven**	5
Two	**Dark Plans For The Remnant**	17
Three	**Village Of The Pig-Keepers**	27
Four	**"Capture Starr Omega!"**	41
Five	**The Shadowland**	49
Six	**Invasion Of The Fields**	63
Seven	**The Prophecy**	73
Eight	**The Martyrs Of The Dome City**	85
Nine	**A Last Resort**	93
Ten	**The Raid**	103
Eleven	**A Whisper In The Night**	113
Twelve	**The Captives**	125
Thirteen	**"I Thee Wed . . ."**	139
Fourteen	**A Command From Goel**	153
Fifteen	**A Church In The Shadowland**	161
Sixteen	**A New Way For Mingo**	171
Seventeen	**A Matter Of Love**	183

Chapter One

Escape From Haven

David and Starr stood beside the fresh mounds of earth. It was a perfect spring day with the blue skies overhead smiling down. White clouds fleecy and fluffy as a flock of sheep moved slowly across the horizon. A spring breeze, soft and gentle and bearing the odors of the newness of earth, came to the pair as they listened to Obadiah pronounce the last words over the fresh graves.

". . . and so, as we commit the bodies of these, our loved ones, to the earth," Obadiah said in a wringing voice, "We proclaim the truth that we shall see them again. For, as the Scripture has so plainly said, 'These must put on immortality'. This morning, we face the grim fact of death. But we anticipate also the glorious truth that the morning will come when we shall all rise, children of the King in a new kingdom."

Starr glanced across at David. She wondered how he could be so calm when he had just lost his parents and his brother in a vicious attack. She had learned, however, in her brief time with the Neo-Crossbearers, or Christians, as she liked to call them now, that death was merely a beginning for the people of the Fields. She studied David's tall form, noting the white scar on his left cheek, the strong jaw line, and the dark hair that waved slightly in the breeze. Then she reached out to take his arm in a comforting gesture.

David turned to face her and smiled. Starr was a tall girl,

although not as tall as he and she looked younger than her age of 24. She had a squarish face with high cheek bones, and an olive complextion. Her auburn hair gave off golden gleams in the sun. The direct gray eyes, sheltered by long, black lashes were calm as he watched her.

"And so," said Obadiah, "We will look to our God to restore all things." Obadiah bowed his head. This tall, prophet-like man, wearing a simple garment of gray, belted by a piece of frayed rope, lifted his voice in a simple prayer. When he was finished, he looked at David and Starr, smiled briefly, and then turned and moved away. David put his arm around his 18-year-old sister, Miriam. Like David, she had black hair and blue eyes. David then put his arm around his brother, Josh, who, at 14 was already tall and well built. He had reddish hair and the same family blue eyes.

The three of them stood there as the villagers came by to offer their condolences. Starr watched, thinking how different it was back in the City. There death was ignored as much as possible and there was never any hint that the living would gaze upon those who had died. A twinge of grief went through her as she thought of the many years she had wasted not knowing that there was a life after death.

After the last of the friends of the family had shaken hands with the three or given them a simple embrace, David turned to Starr and said, "Let's go back to the house. I have something to say."

The four of them went back to David's home and, as they entered, Josh said, with a catch in his voice, "It's not the same without Mother and Father and . . . Timothy."

David comforted his younger brother with, "No, even Christians feel a grief at losing the ones they love. We wouldn't have loved them if that weren't so." David moved over beside the tall, young man, thinking how much Josh resembled their father and said, "We think of it, Josh, as though Father, Mother and Timothy have gone on a long journey that will take them miles and miles away. Then, when we meet them again they will be the same. That's the way it is with Christians. They never say good-bye." David looked up and smiled at Starr who was listening intently. "We always have a meeting coming somewhere in the future."

Josh looked up and bit his lip. "I know, but I'll miss them so much."

"You go right ahead and cry, Josh," David said sympathically. "It's alright. I do it myself sometime."

Miriam interrupted to break the moment, "I'll fix us something to eat." She began to stir in the kitchen and Starr went along to help her.

Soon the two women had prepared a simple meal then called Josh and David to the table. David suggested, "We'll take the food we haven't eaten with us."

Miriam looked at David with surprise, "Where are we going, David?"

"We'll have to leave here." David replied.

"Leave?" Miriam looked surprised. "You mean, leave our home?"

"We'll have to hide." David looked over at her and shrugged his broad shoulders. "They'll be back."

Starr nodded, "That's right. Richard Xi will never give up! He'll have me back one way or the other. As long as I'm here it's a rebuke to the City."

She referred to her former life as a Remedial Historian under the Dome City. The City itself was a modern miracle of technology. After the atmosphere had been polluted on earth, producing a greenhouse effect, the scientists had built a huge, plexiglas, geodesic Dome City—a monstrous, mushroom-like affair. It filtered out the poisonous-like air that had fallen on earth and, inside the Dome City, technology had ruled.

Unfortunately, under the Dome City, men had gone morally

wrong. They had thrown away all concepts of God and had worshipped science and themselves. All the morality and goodness that had been in humanity was shelved and almost forgotten. Starr herself had been one of those who had only a vague dream of a better life.

Starr had discovered that those called the Neo-Crossbearers had a better answer, banned when she had come to the Fields, she gave her heart to the Christ that they served.

The Fields outside the Dome City had been a devastated world for a time. But slowly the earth had refreshed itself until now huge harvests of grain are grown in the Fields. From this grain, alcohol is made which is the primary fuel for the City. She had always thought of the people who lived outside the Dome City in the Fields as Troglodytes, primitive cave men, brutal and ignorant.

Looking around, Starr smiled as she saw how different these people were. The dwellers in the Fields had proven for the most part to be, more gentle and more noble than those under the Dome City. She had joined with them after leaving the Dome City and coming to do a research project. But those in charge had sent Gunships to destroy the village of Haven where she and David were hiding from the authorities. In the attack, David's parents and his younger brother had been killed, along with many Villagers.

Now, David looked at them saying quietly, "It's time to make a plan. We've got to leave this place."

"But where will we go?" Miriam asked.

"A place where the Peacekeepers won't find us."

"Are you so sure they'll come after us?" Miriam looked around the room where she had grown up. "This is the only home I've ever known. The same is true for you also."

"Maybe some day we can come back." David said with compassion in his voice, "But for now, we've got to run and hide. There's no other choice, Miriam."

David sat there speaking quietly, as a grin creased his broad lips. "It'll be hard, but Christ will be with us. As long as we have Him, we have everything."

The Villagers who had survived the attack spent little time preparing to leave. David spoke to them and they looked to him as their leader. He explained that since they were leaving it was likely that, when the Peacekeepers came searching, they might leave those who remained in peace. "But," he said carefully, "You can never be sure. They might destroy everything out of spite."

There was a bustle and quick buzzing noises as the Villagers moved around, gathering their families, talking about what to do. In the end almost all of them decided to leave. Obadiah was a great help. He was, in fact, the pastor of the local Ecclesia, as they called their church. He lent his support to David and when the flock, or the Remnant, as they began to call themselves, came to him, he advised them all, "We had better leave with David. God will lead us to a new home."

All that day there was a flurry of busy work as carts were loaded and animals were gathered for the journey. Starr helped Miriam as she went through the house, taking what few things that could fit in the single wagon that David had insisted on. Miriam and Josh had difficulty limiting their choices.

Josh held up item-after-item saying, "But, I've always had this! Can't I take it with me?"

But Starr and Miriam had finally convinced the boy that he could take only those things that were essential.

Finally the packing was done. Early the next morning they moved out of the ruined village. Almost half the houses had been destroyed by the Gunships of the Peacekeepers. Now there was an eerie feeling about it as the people looked at the ruins.

"We'll come back," Josh said stoutly, "And we'll build those houses. You'll see."

David slapped his brother on his shoulder, "That's the way to talk, Josh! Now, I'm going to depend a lot on you to help, so let's get started."

All day long the small procession wound it's way through the Fields, reaching the foothills of the rising country late that afternoon. David nodded at Starr and Josh who stood beside him, "We'll be able to find cover in those hills. I'll be glad to get out of this open country."

"Can we camp over there by that creek?" Josh asked. "It looks like it might have fish in it."

"That'd be a good place," David nodded. "You go catch the fish while I make the fire. If you don't catch any," he grinned, "I'll throw you in the creek."

Josh smiled for the first time since his family's death. "You just watch! I'll have enough fish to feed us all."

David turned to Miriam and Starr and shook his head. When you're young," he said briefly, "It's easy to bounce back."

"He had bad dreams last night," Miriam said. "I heard him tossing and crying out. He's going to have a hard time adjusting."

David shrugged and his eyes fell. "Aren't we all?" he murmured. "I wish Father were here. He'd be better at this than I am."

Starr at once said, "You're your Father's son. We'll do fine with you as our leader."

David looked at her quickly, then laughed. "Talk to me a lot like that. I need all the encouragement I can get. Well, I'll get the firewood. I'll have to help some of the widows, too, but I'll be expecting a good fish supper."

"Never cook your fish before you catch them!" Miriam laughed. "But, Josh usually comes through."

The camp was soon made and under the shadow of some oak trees, along the bank of a small river, campfires dotted the falling darkness. David went from wagon-to-wagon saying a cheerful word to all, especially to women left without husbands. He understood that they needed more encouragement than others. He noticed also that Obadiah and the Elders of the Ecclesia were quick to offer their help so that soon he was able to return to where Starr and Miriam were cooking fish in a large, black skillet.

"Smells like fish!" David said. He winked at Starr across the fire saying. "They wouldn't be as good as fish I caught!"

"That's what you think!" Josh said. "These are bass. I've got enough for all of us."

"Did you fillet them or have I got to chew through the bones?"

"Why, they were so big, I just filleted them. Look!" Josh held up a fillet of bass. Proudly, he said, "Look, this one must have weighed five pounds!"

"You did good, Josh," David said. He sat down with his back against a tree and the flickering amber light of the fire threw his face into strong relief. As he watched the women move around the campfire, he thought about the difficulties that were to come.

Finally, Miriam said, "Let's eat!" and brought a plate mounded with fried fish to David.

When they all had their plates, they bowed their heads and David said, "Oh, God, we thank You for Your blessings, for this food and for everything that You've given us. Watch over us and keep us safe in the Name of Jesus. Amen."

David sank his teeth into a piece of fish and cried out, "Ow! This is hot!"

"If you wouldn't gobble your food," Miriam said primly, "you wouldn't burn your mouth!" Smiling at Josh she began to pick daintily at the white flesh of the fresh fish. This is good! You're the best fisherman in the family."

"Except me, that is." David winked at her. But he did say, "I couldn't have done any better myself. Let me have one of those potatoes."

Starr raked a baked potato out of the coal and broke it open carefully. "Watch it!" she warned. "It's even hotter than the fish."

The four of them sat there eating with enjoyment. Then they washed down the meal with black coffee from a large blackened coffeepot.

They sat there talking quietly. Finally, Obadiah wandered by. When he was asked to try the fish, he sat down and sampled the food. "This is good," he said. He chewed thoughtfully on a morsel of the fish and then accepted a cup of coffee. Finally he looked at Starr, "How are you, my daughter?"

"I'm fine!" Starr answered, wondering why he had singled her out.

"This is different for you," Obadiah said, studying her carefully. "You grew up in the City."

"Yes, it was all I ever knew."

"It must be very different out here in the wilds."

"I love it," Starr confessed. "I'd hate to think of ever having to live in the City again."

"Tell me about the Dome City," he said. "I've never been there, and from what I've heard, I doubt I'd want to go."

"You'd hate it, Obadiah," Starr said almost vehemently. She began to tell of the City. "It's a technological marvel," she said. "You get in little vehicles and it takes you exactly where you want to go. You don't even steer."

"How does it know how to do that?" Josh piped up, his eyes bright with interest. "You even have to steer a horse or he's liable to take you out in the woods somewhere."

They all laughed and Starr said, "Everything is run by a Megaputer."

"What's a Megaputer?" the boy questioned.

"Well, it's kinda like a mechanical brain, a huge thing. It takes a lot of space and everything in the City is run from it." She went on to explain the system of money. "No one has any money," she said. "You get a certain number of credits and there's a sign in your hand. She held her own hand out, and when Josh stared at it, she shook her head, "You can't see it, but if I held it under a sensor it would identify me and tell how many credits I was being charged."

As she went on to explain, David once broke in to say, "I like life out on the Fringe more than in the City. At least they sound like real people there." He spoke of an area of the City where the Manuals were. They were the ones who kept the City running and did all the hard work. But, they were more like people of the Fields than those who ran the City.

"I like them better. There was a freedom about them which we didn't have in the inner part of the Dome City."

The talk ran slowly around the campfire. A little later on David said, "We'd better get to sleep. It's going to be a long, hard day tomorrow."

Starr and Miriam slept underneath the wagon, wrapped in warm blankets because the nights were cool. Despite the tension that hung over them, Starr found herself sleeping like a baby. She awoke the next day and all day long the wagons rolled into the foothills. The country turned upward, the trees grew heavier, and soon they were following a winding trail beneath green boughs that completely concealed them.

"This is an old trail," David remarked. "I don't know how old it is but I'm glad it's here. When the Gunships fly over, they can't see us."

As they made their way, they paused at noon, ate briefly, rested the animals, then forged ahead. Just before sunset, David found another good camping spot, once again beside a creek.

"Do your stuff, Josh! No wait! I'll come with you," David said. "You come, too, Starr."

The three of them made their way to the creek and David trimmed a sapling and put a line on the end of it. "Here you go! Let's see how big a fish you can catch."

"Here! I kept some worms in the bait can," Josh said. He handed the can to Starr, who stared at it.

"You want me to stick this hook through this slimy thing?" she exclaimed.

Josh winked at his older brother saying, "Well, he's not going to hook himself. Go on! Do it like this."

He showed her how to put the worm on the hook and then the two stood and watched her. Distastefully, Starr shook her head. "I'm not putting that nasty thing on any hook."

"I'll do it for you," Josh said, manfully. He threaded the worm on her hook and said, "Now, just toss it out as far as you can."

Starr obeyed and the bait sank to the bottom. She had watched Josh and David fish and, when the line gave a sudden jerk, she screamed and pulled at it, but it seemed to be hung up.

"You've got a big one," Josh yelled. "Pull him in! Pull him in!"

Starr tugged as hard as she could and slowly backed away from the creek. Then, something came up to the surface, an awful looking thing. She screamed and dropped the pole, "What's that!"

Josh leaped forward, grabbed the pole and tugged on it. He pulled out a big turtle, armored with a vicious-looking beak.

"It's a turtle," he said. "Oh, boy! Turtle soup tonight!"

"I'm not eating any of that old thing!" Starr protested.

But as it turned out, she did. They caught enough fish but Josh was proudest of the turtle. He cleaned it and, when Miriam made it into a soup, Starr was finally persuaded to test it. To her surprise it was delicious.

"Ummmmm! I don't see how anything so ugly could taste so good!"

"Hard to beat turtle soup," David nodded. He carefully tasted the steaming hot broth, blew on it and then put it into his mouth. Chewing thoughtfully he said, "I don't know whether it tastes the most like chicken or fish, but it sure is good."

They sat around the fire and Starr thought how nice it was to have a family.

"You know, I didn't have a family in the City." She smiled at the three and said, "It's good to have brothers and sisters."

David gave her an odd look. "Well, I'm not exactly your brother," He said. "Matter of fact, I intend to be a lot more than that."

Starr flushed for she was still easily embarrassed by references to their coming marriage.

"I think it's exciting, you two getting married," Miriam said. "You won't have a very pretty dress, though, to get married in."

"Marriage is more than a dress," David said loftily. "Besides, Starr would look good in a feedsack."

"I hope you pay nice compliments like that after we're married," Starr smiled.

Soon Josh grew sleepy and then Miriam, eyeing the happy couple said, "I think I'll go to bed myself."

After the two had gone, David and Starr sat staring into the fire. He moved over and sat beside her, saying, "There might be a bear out in the woods. I'd better move in close to protect you." He put his arm around her and drew her near him. When she turned to protest, he squeezed her, and without warning, kissed her lovingly.

Starr enjoyed the kiss. She put her hand up behind his head and drew him closer, her lips responded to his kiss. There was something about David's strength that she needed. (She had been taught that a woman should be strong, but that was a fable.) As Starr held him, she was aware that she needed his strength as much as he needed her gentleness and submission. Pushing away, she said, "That's enough."

"I thought I would be the one to say when enough is enough," he grinned. He poked the fire with a stick, then tossed the stick in and watched it ignite. "What's marriage like in the Dome City?"

"There's no such thing," Starr said. "There are Loving Contracts."

"What's that?"

"Oh, two people agree to live together as friends. They're called Loving Friend Contracts."

"How long do they last?"

Starr shrugged, thinking about how she had once considered such a thing and now it was distasteful. "Sometimes a month, sometimes six months and hardly ever over a year."

David reached over and pulled her close, "How about a Lifetime Loving Friend Contract?" he whispered.

Starr looked up at him and felt her heart feel light, "That's exactly what I had on my mind." Then she reached up and kissed him again.

Chapter Two

Dark Plans For The Remnant

Richard Xi had been on one of his rare excursions to the outer realms of the Dome City. He now moved back from where the Border Guards were kept alienated from the rest of the populace. As he moved by, a tall, lean man with blonde crew-cut hair, wearing the coarse jacket and heavy boots of the guards, leaned in a doorway marked Service Entrance. He curiously glanced at the Manager of the White Tower as Xi shot him a suspicious look.

These Border Guards aren't to be trusted, he thought sullenly. *There's no way to tell which way they'd go in case of a revolt.*

It was not unusual for Richard Xi to be suspicious. That was part of his nature and also a part of his responsibility as Manager of the White Tower. He had been a suspicious child and adolescent. Then a suspicious young man. Now, at the age of forty, his eyes were like a ferret. He was also slim and quick-moving like a ferret.

He entered a vacuum tube and sat down in a seat attached to the walls. An attendant closed a sliding bar around him and suddenly he was zipped upward one hundred feet where he stepped out into a sled-like affair. Sunlight and the brighter light of the full moon could gleam through the long slow curve of the roof. Now the thick acrylic panels allowed only a muted luster. The black walls of the buildings and the narrow canyons between them stretched endlessly below him in angular swatches of shadow and light. There was little movement in these early morning hours. The City that lay beneath had a vast darkened stillness to it.

Reaching the final station, Xi embarked onto the platform. Most citizens of the City avoided the White Tower. It was a place of fear for most of them. But, as Xi crossed to the Tower itself, he felt a glow of satisfaction. He passed through two rigid security checks, then walked over a smoothly-polished corridor to a room hidden in the interior of the building.

When he stepped inside, he found himself in a narrow, blinding white room. At once his underlings, all wearing white linen uniforms with a single emblem of the Tower itself over their left breast, jumped to attention. "I want a meeting at once. Call all the superior officers to my office!"

Xi disappeared behind a door that opened soundlessly and hissed closed behind him. His own office was not particularly large. It did have one window that allowed a slight glow to permeate the space. He sat down behind his desk on the hard-back chair and waited, his face impassive.

Soon the door opened again and six men filed in and aligned themselves before the desk of Richard Xi.

"We're all here, Sir," the leader said (A tall man with white hair and strangely colored green eyes). "What are your orders?"

Richard Xi leaned forward, "My orders are to recapture Starr Omega."

"Starr Omega?" The tall, green-eyed man, Captain MU by name, said uncertainly. "Is this a high priority, Sir?"

Richard Xi shot him a hard glance. "Captain MU, I don't think you understand the seriousness of what has happened. One of our own has defected. Do you think that the City doesn't know about Starr Omega?"

"But, she's only one person," Captain MU protested.

"A revolt and a rebellion *always* begins with one person,

Captain. I'm surprised you don't know your history any better than that."

Captain MU shifted his feet uncertainly. He was a man of tremendous power within the structure of the government, and the only man in front of Xi's desk who was not afraid of him. As a matter of fact, he was relatively sure he would be sitting behind that desk sooner or later. It was his policy to fight subtlety against anything that Richard Xi proposed. Thus, the record later would show that he was right and that Richard Xi was wrong.

"She was only a minor official in a minor department!"

"I'm sure you consider the office of Historical Revision 'minor' but that shows how little you know about power," Xi said grimly. He would liked to have sent Captain MU to the Relievers right away but the man had too many powerful friends. Xi leaned back in his chair and said, "Are you aware that only through controlling the minds of our people do we hold power?"

"Yes, but . . ."

"You need to do your homework, Captain MU," Xi said, enjoying his moment of triumph. "If we let the Underlings know what the past was like, they'd clamor for it again. What we must do is rewrite history so that it agrees with what *we* have decided is best for the people."

"Some would say that untruth is never right," Captain MU argued.

"The people do not need to know the truth. They need what is best for them," Xi snapped arrogantly. He rose to his feet and took several paces, then turned to them. "Their minds would be filled with God and peace and all that nonsense from their Scriptures." His voice rose as he cried shrilly, "I tell you, we're going to stamp out these Neo-Crossbearers and Starr Omega who has become a symbol for them!"

A short, heavyset man with mild blue eyes asked tentatively, "Could you explain why she's so important, Sir?"

"Yes. Starr Omega was one of us. She had the finest education we could give her. She had rooted out all of her romantic ideas of love and had become a Reliever." A Reliever was one who simply put to rest those who were an embarrassment to the State. The Relievers eliminated those who were sick or old or politically incorrect. It was an honored profession in the City.

"If we allow her to get away, it is an admission that our system has failed."

Another of the Lieutenants asked, "How did she manage to escape? I thought no one had ever escaped from the White Tower."

"Her rescuers had help from the inside."

"You mean, there are spies in the White Tower?" Captain MU asked, his eyes narrowing.

"How else could anyone have been snatched from our grasp?" Xi snapped angrily.

"Have the spies been found yet?" MU demanded.

"Our Secret Police are working on it. Rest assured, when we find whoever it is, they will pay dearly."

"Well, what about Starr? Where is she now?" the short man asked quickly.

"She is either in the City, hidden by the Underlings, or perhaps down in the Shadowland."

"That will be a job. There are so many of them." The short, tubby man whose name was Omicron, shook his head sadly. "There are so many, many of them." He repeated. "And, down in the Shadowland—none of us ever go there."

"That is true," Captain MU said. "I have been concerned about that. This Neo-Crossbearer group, when they are detected, flee to the Fringe or to the Shadowland where the Underlings hide them."

"They can't hide them forever. I have a plan to take them. But, my suspicion is that they have fled back to the Fields."

"Why do you think that, Sir?" Captain MU demanded.

"We have evidence that my predecessor was killed by these rebels. Bernard Alpha died a hero's death. He fell into the river trying to apprehend them."

"And was devoured by the Rippers?" Omicron demanded. "What a horrible death."

"Yes, a hero's death, as I said. Now, I am putting you in charge of searching the Shadowland, Captain MU and you, Omicron will search through the Fringe. If Starr Omega and her rescuers are there, find them. I will work on another assumption."

"And what is that, Sir?" MU asked eagerly.

"That will be *my* secret. All dismissed." Richard Xi watched as the troop trudged out and, when they were gone, he pushed a button on his desk. "Get Saul Lambda! Have him brought to me at once."

"Yes, Sir!"

Saul Lambda was enjoying himself at a Sensory Station. The story that unfolded involved sex and violence to an external degree. As he watched it and felt it unfold, he thought to himself, *It must have been pitiful back in the days of movies when all people could do was watch a story.*

Sensory development came when science discovered how to attach electrodes to the temples of an individual which enabled him to feel whatever the story included. As Lambda watched, he enjoyed the sensation of crushing the skull of an enemy as if it really happened. After the gory battle, the story turned to a lovely woman. He felt himself moving toward her, reaching out and smelling the sweet perfume, and feeling the silky texture of her skin . . .

"Lambda! I have a call for you!"

Lambda was infuriated at being interrupted at such a moment, but he knew his clerk would never interrupt him at a sensory unless it was important. Ripping the apparatus from his head, he flung it down and stomped out of the sensory room, down the hall, into his office. "Well, what is it?" he demanded.

"It's Manager Xi. He wants you immediately."

At once the dark, muddy eyes of Saul Lambda narrowed. He was as suspicious as his superior Richard Xi. A call like this could mean trouble. *It could also,* he thought swiftly, *mean a chance for promotion.* Xi had it in his power to raise anyone he chose. Saul Lambda at once asked, "What does he want?"

"He didn't say, Sir. Just for you to get there as quickly as you can."

"You're in charge until I return."

Lambda left his office which was a small cubicle and moved through the White Tower. He was stopped by guards at several check points where he grumpily gave his number and extended his hand for a security check. The White Tower was heavily guarded, it took him fifteen minutes to make his way to the deep recesses where the office of Richard Xi was located.

"He's waiting for you, Lambda," Xi's Lieutenant nodded. "Go right in."

Saul Lambda passed into the white office and found Richard Xi standing before the single window, looking out. From where he stood, Lambda could see down far beneath a few trees and a grassy spot, a park in fact.

Without turning around, Richard Xi said, "Bernard liked to look at that little park down there. I often wondered what he saw in it."

As a matter of fact, Xi knew exactly what Bernard Alpha had seen. Alpha had some heresy in him. Xi had discovered it by reading his secret journal. Now he turned to face Lambda, determined to revenge Alpha who had been a loving friend to him for some time. "I have a job for you," he said abruptly.

"Yes, Sir? What is it?"

"It will require you to leave the Tower and do Field work."

"Field work, Sir?"

"Yes, I am assigning you the task of bringing Starr Omega back. Apprehend her and those that are with her. Bring them back to the City."

"Yes, Sir. I'll need all the information I can get. She's in the Fields?"

"So I suspect." Xi slumped down in his chair and began toying with a pair of steel balls that lay on the table top. He liked to click them together and roll them around in his hands. Especially in times of stress did he tend to toy with these shiny steel balls. They seemed to comfort him and give him some sort of peace.

He looked up and said quickly, "You'll have all the information you need from her files. You've been in the Fields before?"

Lambda hesitated, "Only once on a very brief field trip. Some of my men have been there. I'll get an adequate guide." He hesitated again and said, "How important is this? What priority is it?"

"It is a number one priority," Xi snapped. "I want this woman brought back!"

"Alive?" Lambda asked cautiously. The answer, he knew, would tell him something about the mind of Richard Xi.

"Yes, alive." Richard Xi rolled the balls in his hands furiously making the only sounds in the quietness of the room. "She must be publicly disgraced, then executed."

"I will have her. I'm to be given a free hand?"

"Ask for whatever you need. Get on with it."

"Yes, Sir." Lambda turned, went to the door. He was stopped when Xi raised his voice.

"Lambda! Be sure you don't fail. If you fail, the results could be disastrous."

"And if I succeed?" Lambda smiled suddenly, his thick, brutal lips turning upward. Lambda was a short, muscular man, physical in the extreme. He looked very much like a wrestler back in the old days, his head mounted on a mount of muscles as though he had no neck.

Xi studied the man carefully. As always, he was suspicious of those with ambition and Lambda had enough ambition for a dozen Caesars. *I'll have to watch him,* Richard Xi thought. *Like many others, he would be after my job.* "If," he said carefully, "You are successful, you will be richly rewarded, Saul."

The piggish eyes of Saul Lambda gleamed, "That's kind of you, Sir, but then you're always faithful to your subordinates."

Richard stared at him, looking for any sign of sarcasm. But Lambda was to good an actor.

"On your way, then," he said. "Be quick!"

Lambda left the office of Xi and returned to his own. For an hour he sat in his chair, staring at the blank white wall. He was a thick man physically, but very sharp mentally. Finally, he pressed a button on his intercom saying, "Send me Leo Zeta."

It was only ten minutes after his command that the door opened and a fat man entered the room. He had pale blue eyes and a narrow slash of a mouth. "You sent for me, Sir?"

"Yes, sit down. We have to make plans."

Leo Zeta was what would have been called a "hit man" in the days of gangsters back in the Twentieth Century. Whenever Richard Xi wanted someone to disappear, he passed the message to Saul Lambda and Lambda always turned to Leo Zeta to get the job done.

Zeta sat listening and, when Saul Lambda finished, he asked one question. "You want the woman alive?"

"Yes, it has to be that way."

Zeta said sternly, "If I were in Richard Xi's seat, I would wipe out everyone in the Fields."

"Then you'd be a fool, Zeta!" Lambda snapped. "How do you think this City runs? On the fuel we get from the grain they grow.

If they all died, we'd die, too. Don't try to think, Leo," he said abruptly. "Just do what I tell you!"

Zeta was a thick-skinned individual. Insults, when they were rarely given, simply rolled off his back. "I'll need Gunships and a big force," he said.

"You'll have all you require. Get your group together and put your plan on paper. Bring it to me for my approval."

"Is it just the woman we don't kill?" Zeta demanded.

Saul Lambda shrugged, "You can't carry out an operation like this without trouble," he said. "If a few of the Primitives get killed, it doesn't matter. There are always more of them. They breed like rats," he said.

Zeta rose to his feet. "I'll see to it, Sir."

When Zeta had left, Lambda stared at the picture that he called up on his computer, a picture of Starr Omega. He studied her features, shook his head and then smiled grimly. "I hope you are enjoying your vacation in the Fields," he whispered softly. "You won't be enjoying it much longer!"

Chapter Three

Village Of The Pig-Keepers

Josh was wandering through the stalls in the center of the small village when he heard a sound overhead. Looking upward, he searched the skies quickly then cried out, "Look, Miriam, Gunships!"

Miriam had two large bunches of carrots in her hands. She had been bargaining with the vendor, a tall, saddle-faced man with muddy brown eyes and a twisted mouth. She quickly handed the carrots back to the vendor and, despite his protest, walked away. She was followed by Josh who kept his eyes on the specs that were growing ever larger. "Do you think they're gonna blast this village like they did ours?" he asked nervously.

"I don't think so," Miriam said, "But they're looking for Starr and David. I'm pretty sure of that."

"What are we going to do? Maybe we'd better go tell everyone so we can run for it."

"No," Miriam said decisively. "Let's wait a moment. They're not looking for us so let's wait and see if we can hear anything that might help us."

The two melded into the crowd of villagers that had gathered to watch the Gunships descend. They were awed by the massive size of the Gunships. Painted dead black, they seemed like huge, monstrous spiders as they descended from the sky and settled down on the earth sending towers of dust high into the air. The propellers slowed to an even cadence, throbbing and sending more dust into the air. A door was lowered and men clothed in white uniforms and carrying weapons poured out.

"Gosh," Josh whispered, "There's a lot of them, aren't there?"

"Don't say anything, Josh." Miriam whispered. "Just listen and see what we can hear."

The Peacekeepers threw a circle around the village, their white uniforms spotless and glistening in the bright morning sunshine. They wore reflective visors over their eyes making them look less than human. The weapons they held in their hands looked simple. But they were far more deadly than the villagers could even suspect.

A tall man in a white uniform with a gold bar on the top of his helmet stepped forward. His voice was evidently amplified, for it boomed out over the morning air, startling the villagers.

"Remain where you are. Be still and you will not be harmed. Where is the Chief of your village?"

A short, pudgy man wearing a faded blue shirt and trousers of the same material stepped forward. He looked dazed as he moved forward to stand before the Captain.

"What is your name?" the Captain barked.

"Samuel."

"Alright, Samuel. I'll have some answers from you."

"Y-yes. Yes, Sir. Y-yes, Sir. Anything."

The abject countenance of Samuel was enough to satisfy the Captain. "We're looking for two fugitives, maybe more. Are there strangers in your village?"

Samuel shook his head instantly. "No, Sir."

There was a silence and the Captain stared at the small man. "Look over this crowd! Do you know all these people? Are they all of your village?"

Samuel turned and let his eyes drift over the crowd. Josh was standing in direct line with him, he felt a shiver go up his back for

Samuel's eyes picked him out. Josh knew well that these small village Mayors, or Chiefs, knew everyone in their vicinity. He fully expected Samuel to point his finger and say, "There! Get that one! I don't know him." But he did not.

"No, Captain. No strangers here. These are all my people."

"You're sure of that?"

"I've known them all since they were born," Samuel insisted, nodding emphatically. "Who are you looking for? Maybe they'll come in later."

"It's a man and a woman." The Captain gave a perfect description of Starr and David, then said, "We'll be back again. If we learn that you're harboring them the same thing will happen to your village as happened to Haven."

"You can trust us, Captain," Samuel said. "Isn't that right folks?" He turned around and nodded. A murmur of agreement went over the people.

"We'll have a look around, just to be sure you're not lying." He turned to look at the Peacekeepers, "Alright, spread out. Go through every house."

The Peacekeepers immediately broke their ranks and began to search through the village. They were coldly efficient, entering every doorway, scattering furniture and doing the same with the businesses. It did not take long and Josh had plucked up his courage enough to edge closer to the Captain who stood with his arms across his chest. Samuel the Mayor said, "If you have any pictures of them, that might help."

The Captain turned his mirror-like visor toward Samuel. "Very well. There will be a large reward, you understand, Mayor. You can distribute it as you please."

"Oh, that would be wonderful."

Samuel took the two pictures that the Captain had produced out of an inner pocket of his uniform. He stared at them for a moment, then looked up and said blandly, "I shouldn't forget these two. I'd certainly like to have some of that reward."

"There's plenty to go around. We're putting the word out all over the country that whoever turns up this pair won't have to worry about anything for a long time."

"You ought not to have any trouble," Samuel said. He glanced over to the Gunships and said, "Why, you can cover the whole territory with those things. I guess you can see everything when you get up in the air, can't you?"

The Captain shoved his visor up and put his pale blue eyes on Samuel. "No, we can't. They can hide in groves of trees, canyons, and in caves. That's why we're offering the reward. What's over that way?" he said.

"That way? Oh, they wouldn't be over there. That's the Badlands. You know about that."

"Not very nice country?"

"No. Now, over there," Samuel said, pointing in another direction, "Plenty of woods, trees, fresh water, and game. They could live there forever. You'd have to go in and hunt them down with dogs. Take a long time, but that's probably where they are."

The Captain rubbed his eyes and shook his head, "I suppose you're right." He looked up and saw his men milling around and called out sharply, "Alright, get aboard! We haven't got all day!"

Josh watched as the white-clad Peacekeepers climbed rapidly into the Gunships. The rotor blades picked up speed and the black ships rose abruptly into the air. They wheeled around like large dragonflies and headed in the direction where Samuel had pointed.

Samuel looked over and winked at Josh. "I guess they didn't get much off us that time, did they, Son?"

"No, Sir, they didn't."

"Now, don't tell me anything," Samuel said. "I don't want to know. In case they come back, I won't have to lie. If you run into anyone who is interested, you may pass it along that the ships have gone off to the west. If I were a fugitive, what I'd do is head on to the Badlands. I don't think they'll be looking very carefully around there."

Josh stared at him and a grin came to his lips. "If I see anybody who is interested, I'll tell 'em. Thank you, Sir."

"God bless you, my boy," Samuel said. "May the Lord watch over you and any friends who might need help."

Josh ran at once to where Miriam was standing. "Come on," he cried, "We've got to get back to the camp! I've got something to tell David."

"I sure wish those Peacekeepers were looking here and we could hide over in a better part of the world," David grunted. He and some of the other men had been lifting a wagon out of a crevice the wheels had fallen into. The land was little better than a desert. Here and there was an oasis of green trees and occasionally a spring of water that made an emerald spot in the cracked earth. But mostly, it was desert.

Starr came over and said, "Still, I'd rather be in a desert away from those Peacekeepers."

"Yes, you're right." David grinned at Josh and said, "You did mighty fine finding out about those Peacekeepers, Brother. I think I'm going to make you a permanent scout."

Josh ducked his head. He liked it very much when David praised him. Now he said, "Where are we going? We're about out of food." They had been on the trail for three days. The children were crying for water which had been rationed to little more than a pint a day.

"Over there!" David said.

"I seem to remember this country. We were in it once."

"Yes, that's the Village of the Pig-Keepers."

Starr wrinkled up her nose. "They were nice but, the whole village smelled like a—like—like a—"

"Like pigs!" David grinned. "Well, we don't smell too good ourselves. The one thing they have got in this village is good water. If we make it, we can take baths and rest the animals. Come on, let's try to make it before nightfall."

They did not make it that night. The animals were too tired and thirsty and David hated to punish them. He called for a camp and they made a dry camp that night. However, the next morning they left before dawn, and by ten o'clock had reached the Village of the Pig-Keepers.

"It doesn't smell any better," Starr said.

"Can't help that," David said, "But at least we can get rested."

They were met at the outskirts of the village by a small committee. The Pig-Keepers were cut off from most of the world. They raised their animals, lean ugly-looking boars and sows armed with sharp teeth. They were clannish people and had little to do with the other villagers—or the other villagers had little to do with them!

However, one of them, David greeted warmly. "Hello, there Punch." he said.

Punch, a tall, skinny man with sunburned skin and a batch of orange-red hair grinned. "Well, it's you again! Come on your vacation?"

The two men shook hands and David turned, "You remember Starr Omega? We were here a few months ago."

Punch turned his pale blue eyes toward Starr and nodded, "Why sure. I had to knock a few of our fellows in the head to save you, if I remember."

Starr laughed at the memory. "Yes, you did, Punch," she said, "And I've always been grateful."

"Of course you have," Punch nodded. "Who'd want to go around with a scruffy pair like that—when you could have a fine looking chap like me!"

Josh and Miriam were staring at the man who was about as

homely as a human being could be. Still, when he turned his eyes on them and studied them, there was a friendliness in him.

"Who's this bunch you've got with you, David?" Punch questioned.

"Did you hear about Haven?"

"Haven? Your village? No, what about it?" Punch listened as David explained how the Gunships had destroyed it. When he mentioned the death of his family, Punch shook his head. "Sorry to hear that, old boy, really sorry."

"They're with the Lord now," David said solemnly.

"Yes, indeed. Yes, indeed." Punch nodded. He had no teeth, so his sharp chin almost met his nose when he closed his mouth. He looked at them, then spoke, "We had a few visitors here."

"Peacekeepers?" David asked quickly.

"Yeah, they didn't land in force. One of the ships came down and an officer came in. Funny thing," he said dryly, "The description of the two they're looking for could be you and Miss Starr Omega here."

David stared at him and then smiled, "I suppose lots of people look like us."

"No doubt! No doubt!" Punch said. "Everyone's hot and thirsty. Let's get some food down you." He looked around then asked, "Anyone hungry?"

"I am!" Josh piped up.

"From the looks of you, you must be the brother of this ugly fellow here." Punch nodded toward David. "Well, I've got a special treat for you, young fellow." He licked his lips and nodded firmly. "Pig lips, fried pig lips! How's that sound?"

Josh stared at him and swallowed, "It sounds good to me." He said bravely. "I'll eat anything you will."

Punch broke out into a high cackle of a laugh. "Good enough," he said. "Come along."

Two hours later, Starr and David and the others felt better.

They had eaten something better than pig lips and drunk until they could hold no more. Now David and Starr, along with Josh and Miriam, sat in the cool recess of Punch's clay house. It looked horrible, but the thick walls of clay shaded a cool interior.

David had decided long before that Punch, despite his homely appearance and aggressive manner, was a man to be trusted. "We've got to hide out, Punch," he said. "They're gonna be searching everywhere—for a while anyway."

"Well, it can't be here," Punch said. "Not everyone's the gentleman that I am." He winked broadly at Miriam and added, "A young lady like you has lots of young gentlemen admirers, I suppose."

Miriam blinked in surprise, then flushed. "Not all that many," she said quickly.

Punch leaned back and studied her, then shook his head sadly. "I know you're taken with me," he said. "I could tell that from the time you first laid eyes on me. But I'll have to be honest with you, I'm already spoken for."

Miriam swallowed a laugh and tried to look disappointed. "Well, Mr. Punch, I've found out that the good men usually go first. It's my hard luck, I suppose."

"Don't worry. I've got a young brother who's even better looking than I am. I'll introduce you to him later on."

"Thank you," Miriam said. "I would appreciate it."

Starr could not tell if the grotesque Punch was in earnest or not. She suspected that behind his banter lurked a sharp, keen mind so she asked, "Punch, what are we going to do? How can we hide?"

"I've been thinking about that." Punch picked up an earthen jug and poured some pale liquid into a large mug. Peering into it he said, "This is a new batch. I don't know if it's any good or not."

David tasted it and found it to be the most fiery drink he'd ever had. He said nothing. Punch lifted his mug, took a swallow and his eyes opened in surprise. "This is fine. But, it's only the first sip. Let's see how it goes." He took three or four big swallows, his Adam's apple bobbling up and down in his throat, then paused for breath. "Ahhhh!" he said. "Not bad, but is it good all the way to the bottom?" He gave them a hard look. "One can't trust these things." He lifted the mug again and did not stop until the mug was empty. Putting it down, he wiped his lips on his sleeve then asked, "How are you going to stay hidden? That's the question."

"That's the question," David smiled. "You have any answers?"

"What you need," Punch said in a meditative fashion, "Is a chap who knows these hills and canyons like the back of his hand." He waved his skinny hand, and said, "Someone who knows where the water is, where the fruit is, and where the game is. That's what you're needing, David, old boy."

"Do you know such a man?"

"Why, I was thinking I might do a turn myself." Punch leaned back in his chair, laced his skeletal fingers together and said, "There's not much going on here in this little place. Haven't had to beat anyone for days now. Not much manhood left. Not like the good old days." He winked at Miriam and nodded. "You won't find much that would be suitable for you," Then he grew serious and brought his chair forward. "I'd say it would be best if we got out of here at once. There's a reward out and not everyone in this place is as noble or honorable as your Host."

"Would you do that, Punch?"

Punch looked at Starr and said, "It'll be a picnic."

"How soon should we leave?"

"Quick as we can. They'll try to follow us, of course, for the reward. I'll lag behind, sort of a rear guard, and discourage such activities."

"We're in your debt, Punch," David said with affection. "I

know you won't take money, but perhaps we can make it up to you some day."

"Perhaps you can," Punch replied airily. "In any case, it'll be a picnic."

It was to be an odd sort of "picnic" for the Remnant. Two days later, Punch led them out of the Village early in the morning. They were rested and fed and some of them wanted to stay.

"Nope! Those Peacekeepers, they'll be back. Can't stay here!" Punch said cheerfully. "But come on, we'll be alright."

"He always looks on the bright side of things, doesn't he?" Starr asked David as they followed behind the lanky guide.

"He's a fine chap. Not like some out here in the Badlands. It's pretty much a rough crowd."

Punch led them through a maze of canyons and broken land. At night they stopped twice, each time near a water hole with plenty of clear water for the cattle and for drinking.

In the evening of the third day, however, he said, "Tomorrow we'll be at a place where we can take a few days. Big cave can't be seen from the air. Good water, too." Punch said as he ate a juicy piece of rabbit that he had gotten with his slingshot. He was a phenomenal shot with the thing and was teaching Josh the same skill. "Not bad for a rabbit," he said. "Nice and juicy." He licked his fingers and nodded. "I'll be leaving you for a little while, a few days."

"Where are you going, Punch?" David asked in alarm. "We'll be lost out here!"

"Oh, I won't be gone long, but it occurs to me that I might be of some help to the Peacekeepers." When they looked at him in shock he said, "I've got an idea they're going to come back and check all the villages out here. When they do, they'll be wanting a guide, won't they? And who knows this country better than old Punch?"

David smiled at the guile in the eyes of their guide. "Be sure you don't get them lost," he warned.

"Lost? No, I wouldn't do that! I've never been lost in my life out here." He took another bite of the white meat of the rabbit and then looked over at Miriam and winked, "Of course, I've been confused about three days at a time, more than once . . ."

The Peacekeepers had given up on trying to spot the fugitives from the air. Now the Captain was stumbling over broken rock and shale in the track of the skinny guide who had volunteered to lead them.

"Are you *sure* this is the right way?" the captain asked. Looking around the barren, acrid country side, he shook his head, "I don't think a snake could live out here."

"Oh, yes," Punch nodded confidently, "Lots of snakes! Be sure you don't step on one. They're called 'three steppers'."

"Three steppers?" Asked the Captain, his face red with the blazing heat of the sun and his feet killing him because of blisters after the two day steady march into the desert. "Why do they call them 'three steppers'?"

Punch shrugged, "Because if one of them bites you, you've got about three steps to get help. After that, of course, you're dead."

The Captain looked about nervously and the six men with him did the same. They were still wearing their white uniforms which were far too heavy for this kind of work. The Captain had been "set off" at the Village of the Pig-Keepers by Gunship and had accepted Punch's offer to lead them through the likely spots where fugitives might be.

Punch announced, "No water tonight, but maybe tomorrow."

"No water!" the Captain cried in alarm. "Why, we'll die out here without water!"

"Oh, no, we can suck on a piece of that cactus over there."

The Captain looked at the tall form of a cactus filled with sharp spines. "I'm not sucking on that thing," he said. "Look here, fellow, how much farther is it?"

Punch looked down at the ground, then pulled off his hat. His flaxen colored hair hung lankly over his shoulders. "Well," he said solemnly, "If we have luck, and nobody gets snakebit, and if we don't get attacked by varmints, I figure—oh, maybe three days."

The Captain's face turned pale. "Three days!"

"Captain, we can't go on like this!" One of the soldiers, whose lips were chapped and cracked, could barely speak. They were badly dehydrated and he shook his head miserably. "We'll have to get horses!"

"That's an idea," Punch nodded. "Except, they don't do too well out here either. The Painters like them too much."

"Painters? What do you mean, Painters? Who's going to paint out here?"

"Painters! Lions! Real bad in this part of the world. They love nice juicy hoss flesh—man flesh, too. Didn't you hear 'em howling last night?"

"I did hear 'em," the Captain said. He held his gun more tightly and made a decision. "We can't go on like this."

"Why, Captain, we'll catch up with those folks," Punch argued. "Just trust old Punch."

"I'll trust you to get us back to that village," the Captain said grimly. He turned and walked back down the trail. He did not see the gleam in Punch's eyes and, when they finally staggered back into the village, he was only able to gasp over his radio, "Pick us up! Pick us up!"

"Did you apprehend the fugitives?"

"No. We can't take 'em like this. There has to be another way."

Shortly after dawn Punch appeared back at the camp of the Remnants. He regaled them with his stories of the patrol and said, "Don't reckon they'll be coming out this way. You'll be safe for a little while."

Afterwards, David said to Starr, "It's good to have a friend like Punch. A person doesn't have many like that, I guess."

"He's a good man. He looks awful, but I guess you and I have learned not to trust what things look like, haven't we, David?"

"Oh, I don't know. I kinda like what you look like!" They were standing alone beside the spring and he leaned over and pulled her close. He kissed her cheek and said quietly, "This is hard, but somehow one day we'll be out of it. The Lord is going to see us through this."

Chapter Four

"Capture Starr Omega!"

Richard Xi had been nervously pacing the floor. Saul Lambda had appeared unannounced, and the news he brought was not good.

"A matter of time?" Xi whirled and glared at Lambda. "Time is the one thing we don't have, you fool," he snapped sharply.

Lambda shifted unconsciously. A hard man himself, he found it difficult to take criticism, even from such a powerful figure as Richard. "I don't see what the rush is. We'll have them within a week, two at the most."

"That's what you said last week and the week before that!"

Lambda shifted uncomfortably. He put his strong hands behind him, clasped them, then gritted his teeth before answering. "You don't know that country out there! It's barren, filled with caves, canyons, mountains and not much grass or trees. There's no way we can send large forces in on foot."

"What about the Gunships? Just fly over them!"

"That's no good. They could hear the Gunships coming miles away. All they have to do is duck into a cave. The country's honey-combed with them," he said bitterly.

"Can't you get anything out of the villagers? Someone's bound to have seen them!"

"You know how those people are, the Primitives. They hate us. They stick together like glue."

"What about the reward?"

"I thought that might help," Lambda admitted, but shook his head. "So far we've had lots of volunteers, but we're not *sure* they're in the Badlands. They might have gone east, hiding out in the forest. That's a big country out there, Sir. It's not like searching a bedroom!"

"You watch your mouth!" Xi said sharply. "If you can't do the job, there are others who would like to have a try at it. It's time you earned your keep around here."

The argument went on for some time and finally Richard Xi said, "Get that woman and get her quick or I'll find somebody else!"

"Yes, Sir!"

Lambda left Xi's office fuming. He immediately went at once back to his own quarters where he sat for half an hour, staring at a blank wall, and allowing the rage that rose within him to simmer down. He was a man of violent passions, and had learned long ago that to turn them loose was not always a good idea. "Save it," he murmured to himself, "For when you catch that woman and man . . ."

He took several deep breaths, then poked the button on the instrument in front of him. "Send Zeta in here!" He leaned back, and when Leo Zeta made his appearance, said, "We're in trouble, Leo."

"Is Xi kicking up a fuss again?"

"Yes. He told me either we catch that pair or get sentenced to the Fields."

"Xi better be careful." (Leo Zeta was little more than a brutal hit man for Lambda). There was cruelty in his pale blue eyes as he murmured, "Someday Xi's going to step down—in one way or another."

Lambda stared at the killer. He knew that there was not one ounce of pity or mercy in Leo Zeta. *A useful man*, he thought to himself, *But a dangerous one. Still, if Xi were to be out of the way, I'd be the logical one to take his place.* He studied Zeta carefully and the thought came to him, *And then Leo would be in my place—and expecting to come to an even higher position.*

"Alright," he said. "What can we do? We've got to do something!"

Leo laced his fingers together, then snapped them, making the knuckles crack. He was fat, but under the fat were layers of hard muscle. Men were constantly misjudging him to their sorrow. Lambda had judged him correctly. There was no mercy in him. Finally, Leo said, "I've got an idea."

"What is it?"

"They managed to elude the Peacekeepers. That's because they know that country and the Peacekeepers don't. It would be a different matter if they were in the City. We would run them into the earth in no time.

"So? What's the answer?"

"The Border guards," Zeta nodded firmly. "Those fellows go into the Badlands and the forest all the time. Some of them know that country like the back of their hands."

Lambda nodded, his eyes brightening. "That's an idea. Now, get to it. Promise them anything."

"We may have to get rough," Zeta warned. "Some of those Primitives out there know more than they're saying. If we could put a little pressure on some of them . . ."

"Do what you have to do, Leo. It's my neck and it's yours, too," he added grimly.

Zeta nodded, "And we know how to take care of our own necks, don't we?" The two exchanged a long thoughtful glance and then Zeta left the room.

Will Sigma strolled aimlessly about the camp of the Border guard. It was called a camp, but really wasn't a camp. It was a walled-off area inside the Domed City, just north of the main gate, or the Western Gate, as the guards called it. It contained a one-eighth mile jogging track who's infield was used as a parade ground and physical training area. There was a gym, complete with exercise equipment, steam baths, and four racquetball courts. There was also an obstacle course and a firing range, plus stables for the horses and barracks for the men.

The guards lived with their families in base housing. The barracks used by the new guards was some distance away from that of the regulars. This arrangement was made for convenience as well as a sense of unity for the guards and their families. It also gave the City control over this strategic and potentially dangerous body of men called Border Guards. Every guard on duty knew his family remained under the watchful eyes of the Peacekeepers.

Despite disliking it intensely, Michael Kappa was one of the guards who had learned to adjust to his job. Blonde and crew cut with eyes like gun metal, he was stronger and faster than most men. Unlike most Border Guards, he had a razor-sharp mind.

He had a visitor that day—Lido, one of the City dwellers—a sharp-featured man of twenty-four with keen brown eyes and boyish voice. The two had become friends through Starr Omega. Lido had come to ask what Kappa thought of their chances.

Kappa leaned back against one of the barracks where the two were standing outside and said quietly, "Not much chance for them."

"But, it's so big out there in the Fields!"

"I know, but I also know that the 'powers that be' want them worse than I've seen them want anything for a long time."

"Will you have to help run them down?"

Kappa looked at him without answering. Then he said, "It may come to that."

"But you don't want to, do you?"

"No."

He gave a distasteful look toward the guard tower and said

bitterly, "Not much I can do about it. None of us are much more than slaves to the City fathers."

Lido said with surprise, "You talk like that? That sounds like treason."

"No one is here to tell them. You won't will you?" he grinned.

"No, of course not."

Kappa looked toward the glistening Dome City and shook his head, "I'd like to be out there in the Fields myself."

"Why don't you go?"

"You are naive, Lido," Kappa said pointedly. "A lot of us would like to go, but our families are little more than hostages. They treat us well enough, but we know what would happen if someone deserted. They even keep us in our own separate community so we don't infect the general population with what we know about the world outside the Dome City."

"What is it like out there?"

"Like? It's like the Garden of Eden!"

"What's that?"

"Oh, just a story in an old book," Kappa grinned. "About a nice garden with trees and animals and streams."

Lido looked around and said, "I thought everything was dead and dying outside this Dome City."

"That's what they want you to think."

"I wish . . ."

"Be quiet!" Kappa had seen his superior officer striding toward him. "Get out of here, Lido! I'll talk to you later."

"Michael Kappa?" The speaker was none other than Leo Zeta. He stopped in front of Kappa and waited until the tall, blonde-haired man nodded.

"I have a job for you and a big reward if you can get it done."

"Always interested in things like that," Kappa said easily. He studied Leo Zeta carefully. He knew him by reputation as a merciless hunter who would step on anyone who got in his way. "What's the job?"

"A little hunting. I understand you're good at that."

"I've done my share."

"You know the Badlands and you know the Fields, don't you?"

"I've been there a few times."

"That's not what I hear." Lambda studied the tall broad-shouldered man and found what he saw to his liking. "What I want is a man who knows how to find a trail—then stay on it."

"Starr Omega, you mean?"

Lambda's eyes opened wide. "You are sharp. Where'd you hear about that?"

Michael smiled slightly, "Who hasn't heard about it? Your boss up there getting nervous about letting her escape?"

Zeta's eyes narrowed. "You're a smart one. That's alright. I like smart men. I'm smart myself." He studied Kappa for a brief moment, then nodded as if he liked what he saw, "Take what you need, as many men as you need, then find the woman and the man, too."

"You want them relieved?"

"No! I want them both taken alive!"

"Want them to make a public confession, I take it."

"That's right, and that's all you need to know, Kappa. You think you can do it?"

"That's a big country out there. A man could hunt for a long time and do his best. Any man, and find nothing."

"Do your best. No reason why you shouldn't move up in your organization. Your boss is pretty stupid or he'd have found them already. Maybe you could take his place."

"Too much trouble," Kappa said. "Then I'd have to go to meetings and be told I wasn't doing things right."

"That's the penalty of moving up in the organization. You don't like that?"

"No. I'll go look for the girl and man, too."

"Alright. Request what you need. I'll leave word. Good hunting."

Kappa watched him move away and said under his breath, "Now there's a hard man. I'd hate for him to be on my trail." He turned and walked softly away in front of the barracks, his mind working rapidly. He was not particularly sympathetic toward the Neo-Crossbearers. Yet, over the past months he had grown more and more dissatisfied with his life. Finally, he came to the stables and found his own mount, a tall, black stallion, and patted him on the neck. "At least we'll have a few days away from this place."

The horse lifted his head and made a shrill noise in his throat, as if he, too, would like to get away. Kappa stroked the sleek, black hide thinking, *I'm thirty-two years old and you're the only friend I've got, Blackie.* The thought depressed him and he said aloud, "Something wrong with a thing like that."

Chapter Five

The Shadowland

Philea carefully moved along the Fringe. In some ways it was her favorite part of the Dome City. The main part of the City was hard and filled with scientific improvements; there was a coldness and lack of humanity about it that she did not like. The streets of the Fringe were literally bursting with energy and the excitement of people. As she walked along, everywhere she looked, there was singing. She heard the whine of a trumpet and then the groan of a saxophone as a small band entertained a group. Everyone was laughing and clapping their hands and a couple were doing a dance she had never seen before.

I wish everyone could be as happy as they seem to be, Philea thought. She was a woman of twenty-five and her straight blonde hair and blue eyes were not unattractive, although she was not pretty in the usual sense of the word. She was the daughter of a man called Philemon who had been "relieved" by Starr Omega. Philea had very fine memories of her father and had learned to forgive Starr Omega for her part in his death. As a matter of fact, it was more than that. She had come to love the young woman as a sister, and now, the news that Starr and David were the subject of a massive search by the Peacekeepers disturbed her.

Now she moved along the street and from time to time entered one of the shops. She was always greeted warmly by the shopkeepers—whether they were men or women. Few of them knew she worked in the White Tower, and those in the White Tower had even less idea that she spent her time and her days among the people of the Fringe. It had been Philea who had been primarily instrumental in achieving the freedom of Starr Omega. As one of the trained nurses there she had been able to help David organize a party that had gotten the young woman free.

Philea entered a fruit store and greeted the owner warmly—a short, pudgy woman with a pair of bright blue eyes and rosy cheeks. "Hello, Rosa," Philea said. "You're looking well."

"Yes, I'm all well now." Rosa came over and planted a firm kiss on Philea's cheek. "I was so sick last week. If you hadn't come to help, I think I'd have died."

"Oh, it wasn't as serious as that!" Philea protested.

"Yes, it was," Rosa nodded, the motion sending waves of flesh trembling down her pudgy body. She was a widow with three small children and it had been Philea who had nursed the family through all of the illnesses that such a family is heir to. "You sat beside me many nights," Rosa said. "I'll never forget it and my how you prayed for me." She gave Philea a playful shake. "Where did you learn to pray like that?" she demanded. "I don't really know how to pray."

Philea was embarrassed. She hated to take any credit for such a thing as praying, or any of her other Christian duties. "Your prayers suit God very well, I am sure, Rosa."

"No, they're not pretty like your prayers. All I can do is beg for God to give me things."

Philea laughed. "That's not so, and when you do ask for things, it's mostly for your children. God doesn't care how pretty our prayers are, anyway."

"He don't?"

"Of course not. When little Lewis comes in to ask you for

something, it doesn't matter how pretty he speaks does it? If he needs it and you have it, you give it to him."

"I guess that's right. And you think God is that way with us?"

"I think so. Matter of fact, I think my own prayers are a little bit too ornamented. I'm going to make them simpler and plainer—like yours, Rosa."

Rosa burst into laughter. "No, don't do that," she said. "I like to hear your pretty prayers. Come back. I've got a present for you."

The two women went back into a room off the back of the shop. Rosa picked a garment out of a cabinet. "I made this just for you. Pretty, isn't it?"

Philea took the blue blouse in her hands and looked down at it with delight. Running her hands over the smooth fabric, she said, "Rosa! It's beautiful! I've never seen such a pretty blouse. You made it yourself, didn't you?"

"Oh, yes. You make pretty prayers, I make pretty clothes. Fair enough, isn't it."

At that point Rosa's three children came tumbling in, all of them under seven. They pulled at Philea until she sat down and told them a story. The oldest, Sammy, said, "Tell us another story."

Philea smiled at his demanding tone but sat down and said, "This is a story about a young man who did some very bad things."

"Like me," Sammy said. "I'm always doing bad things, aren't I, Mama?"

"Yes you are. Why don't you be a better boy, like your brother, or sister."

Quickly Philea said, "You listen to the story and then you can tell me about it." She began telling the story of a young man who had a rich father. "And when he grew up he said, 'Give me all the money that I'll have for my inheritance'. So his father gave his son the money."

"Did he buy lots of pretty clothes?" the little girl asked (She had big black eyes like her mother and dark, curly hair). "If I had plenty of money, I'd have a new dress every day."

"Yes, he bought lots of pretty clothes, Sally," Philea said, "And horses and diamonds and jewels. But, he made some very bad friends."

"Were they robbers?" Sammy demanded.

"They did all sorts of bad things and they really didn't like the young man," Philea said. "They helped him spend all of his money and then, when he didn't have any, they threw him out."

"Did he die?" Sally asked, her eyes enormous.

"No, he didn't die, but he nearly starved to death. He had to go live with the Pig-keepers."

"I wouldn't like that," Sally said. "I saw a picture of the Village of the Pig-keepers once. It was real dirty."

"It is. It's not a very nice place," Philea agreed.

"Well, what happened to him, if he didn't die?" Sammy asked eagerly.

"Well," Philea answered. She put her arm around the young man and her voice fell, "He almost died. And finally, he thought about something. He thought about his father who had lots of money and how happy he'd been back home. He said to himself, *I'm going back home. Even my father's servants have more to eat than I do—and better clothes.*"

"I'll bet his father wouldn't like that!" Sammy said. He turned to his brother and said, "Do you like this story, Jimmy?"

"Yes, I like all of Miss Philea's stories. What happened to the young man, Miss Philea?"

"Well, he started home and he was so tired he could hardly make it. Then, when he got almost to his house, there was his father sitting out in the front and his father saw him. He ran to meet him."

"I'll bet he bawled him out, huh?" Sammy said quickly.

"No, he put his arms around him," Philea said with a smile.

"And he kissed him and pulled him into the house and said, 'Fix the best meal you can. Put some new clothes on my son. He's been lost, but now he's home again'."

Sammy said, "He did all that for that mean kid?"

"Yes, because he loved him."

"I like that story," Sally said. "I wish I had a daddy like that," she said wistfully. "Before he died, he was always glad to see me coming, even when I was bad."

Philea's heart went out to the small child. She glanced up to see tears in Rosa's eyes. Putting her arms around the girl, she whispered, "You still have a father, a Heavenly Father," she said quietly, "And he loves you very much. When you do something wrong, Sally, you just have to tell him about it just as you would have told your earthly father."

Rosa turned aside to wipe her eyes with her apron. When she turned back her voice was husky. "You stay and eat with us."

"No, I have to go. I'll be back tomorrow, though. Maybe I'll be wearing this pretty new blouse."

Despite the protest of the children, Philea left the small shop. She was filled with joy as she realized that there were those, like Rosa, that despite the temptation in the City, kept themselves from it. Philea thought to herself, *Rosa's a fine Believer. Some day she'll marry again and some man will get a good wife and wonderful children.*

The thought of the children struck her because she'd wanted children of her own. But so far, she had never married. Although she'd prayed for a husband, God had never sent one. Finally, she smiled and said, "You don't need a husband, you've got a Heavenly Husband. Now! Get on with your work."

It was two hours after Philea had visited many of the widows of the Ecclesia. When she came out of a humble home of a seamstress, she found Michael Kappa waiting for her. "Come along, Philea," he said. "I've been looking for you."

Philea was somehow disturbed. She knew that Michael Kappa was not one of them. She had talked to him often enough about God, but he had not been receptive. Still, he was not as cruel as some of the other Border Guards. She smiled, saying, "Why would you be looking for me, Michael?"

He studied her and a light of humor came to his eyes. "I'm always looking for a good-looking woman," he said.

His compliment brought a flush to her cheek. She shook her head. "I don't need to hear that kind of talk. You can tell that to the girls at the Tavern."

"How do you know I go to the Tavern?"

"I just know, that's all."

"Never seen you there," Michael teased. "Why don't we go there together. Come on, it's not too early for a little drink."

"No, you know I won't do that."

"Well, just a thought." Studying her carefully he thought, *She wouldn't be bad looking if she'd do something with her hair. Pretty eyes and a nice shape. Wonder why she's never married.*

Kappa was not a man to keep his thoughts to himself and, as he walked along beside her, he asked her that very question. "Have you ever been married, Philea?"

"No."

The brevity of her answer made him turn and he said, "You must have had chances."

Philea shook her head but said nothing. Finally, after an uncomfortable silence, she said, "You'll make fun of me, Michael, but I would like to have a husband, a home and children."

"It shouldn't be too hard. I know several young fellows."

"No, I don't want that," she said quickly. "I'm waiting for the Lord to tell me what to do. So far he hasn't told me that I can marry."

This was a new concept to Michael Kappa. He knew the Neo-Crossbearers believed in a god who could not be seen or touched or in any way perceived. It was a puzzlement to him and he pondered on it silently as the two walked down the busy street. The noise of some playing children sang in the air and there was the smell of cooking meat and fresh bread. Dogs ran barking and yapping, something that never happened in the inner part of the City. It was against the rules. Finally he said, "What do you mean, 'the Lord's never told you you can get married?' I thought you couldn't see your God."

"We can't see him with our eyes. He's a Spirit."

"Then how can he tell you anything. Spirits can't talk, can they? They wouldn't be spirits if they could."

Philea had difficulty framing a reply. Michael Kappa was a child of the Dome City. In the City there was no god. He had been rooted out long ago. The only God was man himself and people were taught to worship man, not some nebulous being known as 'God'. Most of the people had so successfully been brainwashed that they scarcely ever thought of god in the old terms. There were rumors of the old religion, but sophisticated people laughed saying, "That's just a myth—just a figment of your imagination!"

"What about it? How does God talk to you?"

"Don't make fun of me, Michael."

"I'm not making fun," he said. "I want to know. You said God hasn't told you that you can have a husband. Does that mean that some day He may tell you." When she nodded, he said, "Well, how will He tell you?"

Philea began to explain, haltingly, how that in her heart there was something that had been there for a long time. She began by saying, "Jesus is the Christ, the Chosen of God, the Son of God. He came to this earth long ago to die for our sins."

"Most of us die for our sins, or of them," Kappa said lightly.

"But Jesus took all of our sins upon Him. Now we don't have to be bound by wrong things."

"What wrong things?" He looked at her and smiled, "You can't have done too much wrong, Philea. Now, I'm a different story."

Philea shook her head. "It's not the degree. God is perfect and He demands that we be perfect."

"I've never known anybody perfect," Michael snapped. He was confused and didn't really like to talk about this yet, the subject intrigued him.

"It's a matter of the heart," she said. "If you had a son, he'd be your son no matter what he did, wouldn't he? Even when he displeased you, he'd still be your son."

"I suppose that's true. But, if he did wrong, I'd have to punish him."

"That's exactly what God does. He chastises us, His children, just as we would chastise our own children."

"It doesn't sound right to me. I believe in what I can see, smell or taste. There's nothing else out there."

Philea did not argue. Long ago she had learned that argument was useless against the mentality of the City. There is only one thing that makes an impact on those who are blinded by the gods of this world. That is love and gentleness. But the city saw little of that.

Finally, when they had come to a turn in the street, Philea pointed and said, "Let's sit down over there. You can tell me why you came looking for me."

"Alright." Kappa sat down beside her and for a while said nothing. There was something troubling him, His face was tight and his lips were drawn together in a thin line. Philea knew that he was not a happy man, despite the fact that he often made jokes. Deep inside he was a man who was searching for more than pleasure. *That's the god of the City,* she thought, *pleasure and it's all gone so quickly!* "What is it, Michael? No one is listening."

Michael stretched out his long legs, clasped his hands together and squeezed them until they grew tight, then released them. "I have a job I have to do."

"Something you don't like, I can see that."

"That's right. I don't like it but I've got to do it anyhow."

"What is it, Michael?"

"They've ordered me to go find Starr Omega and David, the fellow who got her out of the White Tower."

Philea quickly glanced at him. "Are you going to do it?"

He shrugged his shoulders. "What else can I do? They punish our families if we don't do what we're told."

"You have a family? A wife? I didn't know that."

"No, no wife, but I've got parents and a brother and two sisters. They'd pay for it if I refuse to do what they want."

"That's hard on you," Philea said. "You like Starr, don't you?"

"Yes, I do. I like David, too. But, what's a man to do? Let his own family suffer? It's impossible!"

Philea sat there quietly while the big man poured his heart out. She could tell he was disgusted with what he had to do. Finally, she put her hand on his arm and gently said, "We all have to make these decisions. It may be that God is using you in a way you don't even understand."

"God? How could God use me? I don't even believe in Him."

"God is bigger than our ideas of Him."

Her sentence intrigued him and he repeated her words, "God is bigger than our ideas of Him. You know, there's something to that. Everyone's got some kind of idea about God. Some people think He's the moon or sun. Others that He's in a bottle of wine."

"If that's as big as your god is, you don't have much god, do you?"

"I don't know, the sun's pretty big," he said defensively.

"But God made the sun. He had to. God's outside of all this.

But the one thing you need to know about God is," she said hesitantly, "He loves us."

Michael stared at her unblinkingly. "He loves us," he echoed softly. "You know that for sure do you, Philea?"

"Oh, yes. I know it because, before He came into my heart, I really didn't love anyone, except myself."

"That's the way most of us are," he muttered.

"Not when Jesus comes in," she said quickly.

She quietly continued her "witness" as this big man sat on a bench listening intently. When she finished Michael said, "I don't know about these things. I don't ever think about them." This was untrue, because he often thought about them. What she had said made him nervous. He got up and said, "I'll do what I can for Starr and David." Then he turned and walked off.

As Philea watched the tall figure disappear into the crowd she smiled, "God is on your trail, Michael Kappa. Somewhere up ahead you're going to have to meet Him. And, when you meet God, He'll be bigger than anything you ever imagined."

Philea went at once to the Shadowland. This was the strangest of all the sections of the Domed City. Far underneath the City itself was a maze of tunnels containing machinery, compressors, dynamos, generators: all of the devices that brought food and water and air to the Upper World. Those above never thought much of the Shadowland. They breathed the air and ate the food that were the products of the labors of those who kept things running, without a thought. Only a few of the rulers ever found their way beneath. There was a corps that was a bumper zone, more or less, who would descend into the Shadowland to be sure that the orders were given. They themselves felt highly uncomfortable.

As she descended, Philea thought, *It's like going down into one of the old caves far below the earth where there exists stalactites, darkness and caverns that no man has ever seen. No wonder it frightens people*. But to her, the Shadowland was not frightening. She had many friends down there. She went at once to one of them, a man named Mark, his wife Martha and their two sons, Jacob and John. The boys were six and twelve and, as soon as they saw Philea they ran to her and she stooped to put her arms around them. They expected presents and, as always, she fished in her bag and brought out some sweets that she had purchased on the Fringe. "Now," she said, "Put that in your mouth and you won't make so much noise." The boys clung to her as she went inside the small, cave-like apartment. Inside, however, Martha and Mark greeted her with such warmth that she ignored the poor surroundings. The lights came from two florescent bulbs and cast a whitish light over the single room that served as a living room and dining room.

"How are you, Philea?" Mark asked warmly. He was one of the Deacons of the underground Ecclesia, many of which existed in the Shadowland. He was a tall man with prematurely gray hair. His wife, Martha, was a pretty woman of thirty, with a kind face. "Sit down," Mark said. "Join us as we eat."

Philea felt at home in the house of Mark and Martha and she enjoyed the simple meal that Martha prepared. Afterwards, while Martha was getting the children washed and ready for bed, she said, "I have news, Michael Kappa came to see me tonight."

"Kappa?"

"Yes, one of the Border Guards. He's been ordered to find Starr and arrest her."

"And David, too, I suppose?"

"Yes, of course. They know he broke her out of prison. I'm afraid for them, Mark."

Mark leaned forward, "No, we mustn't fear. God is in all of this, Philea. Starr's now one of us and David's a strong man. God is going to use them both greatly."

Philea was weary. Her duties were demanding. She leaned

back and closed her eyes. "I get so tired, Brother Mark," she said. "So tired, and so many of our people are suffering."

Mark looked at her and after studying her thoughtfully said, "You work too hard; I'm afraid things are going to get worse. Every day we have people fleeing the City, coming down to the Shadowlands. Even in our own Ecclesia, we've taken in over a hundred in the past week."

"Who are they, Brother Mark?"

"Oh, they're people who are hunted by the Peacekeepers. They've broken a rule. Some of them are old and are going to be 'relieved'—put to death. They come here seeking shelter."

The two sat there talking. Mark was the kind of man who could comfort people. Soon Martha came back with the boys who begged for a story. Philea told one of the stories from the Bible. When the boys left, Martha came back and sat down beside her husband. She looked across at Philea and said, "Now, when are you going to leave the Tower and come and be with us?"

"I can't do that. I'm of more use there. I hear things sometimes that are helpful."

"Yes, you do. Starr wouldn't be alive today, I don't think," Mark said, "If you hadn't helped her—but it's hard on you."

"The Lord is with me," Philea said simply. "Is there service tonight?"

"Yes." Mark stood to his feet and shrugged. "You'll have to listen to some poor preaching. I'm doing it myself."

"You're a fine preacher," Martha said. "I'll stay here with the children. You can tell me all about it when you come back."

Philea and Mark left. They made their way through underground tunnels. There always was the hum of machinery and lights dimming and growing stronger, the smell of oil, metal and plastic. It was not a beautiful world. Philea said, "Why don't you leave here and go to the Fields? They say it's beautiful there, green trees, water, lakes."

"I'd go in a minute, but God has put me here to serve," Mark said at once. "You know something about that."

"Yes," Philea said quietly. "I guess we'd all like to go where life is easy; but God sometimes puts us where it's very hard."

"It isn't hard, is it, as long as Jesus Christ is within our hearts?" Mark said. He took her arm and said, "Come now. Don't take any notes. I couldn't bear you going over my sermon, Philea."

Chapter Six

Invasion Of The Fields

The peacekeeping force assigned to run Starr Omega and David to ground was impressive. It had been decided by Zeta, after speaking with Kappa, to leave the Gunships out of it.

"You can't sneak up on game if you are riding in a truck," Kappa had said. "If you're going to capture these two you're going to have to be quiet about it." Zeta had agreed and now there were no more than two hundred of the Peacekeepers that were transported across the river to begin their journey. They were all mounted and Kappa was at the head of the procession. He was speaking with the military commander, a Captain named Barnes.

Barnes looked back at the serpentine trail of horsemen and shook his head. "I don't like it. We need five times this many men."

"There are only two of them, Captain," Kappa remarked idly.

"I know, but we've got to cover a lot of ground." The Captain was a small man, sensitive of his lack of size. For this reason he disliked the tall Border Guard who made him feel inferior. He also resented that Kappa knew the territory and would be, in effect, making the decisions.

"I still say we need more men," he snapped.

"Up to you, Captain," Kappa shrugged his shoulders. "It won't matter how many you have if you're looking in the wrong place. A thousand wouldn't help."

"Well, how do you know where to go?"

"I don't. I just know some places that would be good hideouts for small parties. We might look for a month and find nothing."

"Those weren't our orders!" Barnes snapped.

"No, but I hope you made it plain that we're not magicians."

Captain Barnes was burning for promotion. He had determined from the beginning of this assignment that no matter if he had to half kill his men—or indeed, a few of them, they would not come back empty-handed. "We're going to push the men hard," he said. "Don't be afraid."

"They're not used to this kind of life. Peacekeeping's pretty easy compared to being a Border Guard."

"You won't have to look far behind me, Kappa!" Barnes snapped. "Now, let's double the pace."

Kappa grinned behind his hand as the small Captain spurred his horse. He'll kill his animal in two days at that pace, thought Kappa, which was alright with him. He kept his own mount at a steady trot and all that day was amused as Captain Barnes moved up and down haranguing the men, promising them promotions, credits, wine, women, anything if they were only successful.

Later that night, after they had made camp, Kappa said, "Guess I'll go out and have a look around."

"Look for what?" the Captain demanded suspiciously.

"Might run across some sign of them." Repeated Kappa. "That's what I'm here for, isn't it? Unless you want to go."

Barnes face reddened, "Be back in time. I want to start at sunlight in the morning."

"Right."

Actually, Kappa was certain that neither Starr nor David were within many kilometers of the present location. He was also aware that Will Sigma, a close friend of his, would be on duty at one of the outposts. Two hours later he rode in and was greeted by, "Who goes there?"

"Just me, Will. Michael Kappa."

Will Sigma stepped out of the trees, a tall sandy-haired man with a reddish-blonde beard. He was carrying a shotgun, but lowered it and smiled as he said, "You're off your beat, aren't you, Michael?"

"Well, you haven't heard. I'm the new General in this army. Got anything to eat?"

"Sure—shot a deer this afternoon. Ought to be about right by now."

The two men sat around the campfire eating deer steak and Kappa outlined his mission.

Sigma shook his head. "I like those people, Starr and David. Too bad. I don't guess you'll have any trouble running them down."

"Why, I don't have any idea where they are," Kappa said innocently. "Do you?"

Sigma looked up quickly and saw the humor in the big man's eyes. His mouth turned upward in a grin. "I suspect," he said slowly, "They might be there in the Lake Country. Lots of good places to hide out there."

Something in the way Sigma gave the news alerted Michael Kappa. He turned immediately and looked in the other direction toward the Badlands and, when his gaze returned to the smaller man, he said, "I expect you're right. We'd better have a look over that way."

The two men talked for some time. They had much in common. Sigma hated the Dome City, never going unless he had to. Sigma and Kappa had the manner of old soldiers who had campaigned together—which indeed they had.

"What's going to happen, Michael?" Will asked. He tossed the bone he'd been gnawing on into the fire, sending a column of sparks swirling upward, then said, "The whole thing's on a razor's edge. All it'd take would be a revolt down in the Shadowland and the City would be helpless."

"That's what they're afraid of," Michael nodded. "No one up top could keep the thing going. It's the Shadowland people who know what makes things work. They're the plumbers and electricians. It would all go 'clunk' if it wasn't for them."

"But they'll never rebel. They don't know how much power they've got."

"All they need," Kappa suggested, "Is for someone to tell them. I've often thought that was the way it would go. The real power lies with them and the Primitives out here in the Fields." He waved his hands vaguely toward the north. "If they stop growing grain and making alcohol, the whole thing would grind down. No power without that."

"Still, the Peacekeepers have the guns and they're a pretty rough outfit."

"That's right." Kappa sat there quietly, then remarked, "I was talking to Philea a few days ago."

"Nice girl." Will looked at him and smiled. "You courting her?"

"No, nothing like that. I like her though. Haven't met anyone like her."

"Be careful! That's the way a fellow winds up getting married."

"What could I give a woman," Kappa said bitterly. "Anyway, all she talks about is God."

"That's the way with these Neo-Crossbearers," Sigma agreed. "They're haunted by this idea of a God who loves them—loves everybody."

"That's just it. How could God love a fellow like me. I've done everything you might want to make a list of. Not much of it good. How could he love me?"

Sigma stared at him. "Are you beginning to believe what they say?"

"I don't know. I've never believed anything."

"That's about the way I've been," Sigma nodded. "Still," he muttered and pulled a pipe out of his pocket and lit it up, watching the blue smoke drift upward, he said, "There's something to these people. I don't know what it is."

"I don't either. Some of them are pretty wimpy, I guess. Not David. He'd take that shotgun and make you eat it if he'd take a mind to."

"That's right. Some of them are pretty tough. You thinking of joining them, Michael?"

"Not me! Not me, Will. We're too smart for that, aren't we? Sooner or later, Richard Xi's gonna throw enough Peacekeepers out here to cover the earth. They've got no chance, Starr and David." Michael suddenly looked at him and said, "If you see them, you might warn them."

"I'll do that."

Kappa stayed for a short while, then returned to the camp.

"Well, did you find anything?" Barnes demanded.

"Talked to a fellow. He thinks they might be over there in those big woods. We'll start looking first thing in the morning."

"alright. Think I'll go to bed."

"We're moving at sunrise. I want that woman caught, and the man, too!"

But the Remnant were not in the wooded country. Sigma well knew this and took it upon himself to take a trip to the Badlands. It took several days hard travel and his horse was tired. Finally, he located the Pig-keepers and from there on it wasn't hard to follow the trail. Only a skilled Border Guard such as himself could have done it; he finally came around the corner of a canyon where a rock zipped by his horse, making it rear. "Better turn around!" a voice cried out.

Will got the horse pulled down, pulled his shotgun quickly, and looked at the tall, skinny man who stood, holding a slingshot. "What's wrong with you?" he said angrily. "You could have hit my horse! Or me!"

"If I'd wanted to hit your big head, it would have been easy."

Will looked at the tall, skinny man with the scrunched up face and said, "I'm looking for some friends of mine."

"Turn around and go back where you come from or I'll punch you out."

Will smiled at the fellow. *He's got nerve*, he thought. *I've got a shotgun and all he's got's a slingshot.*

"Don't want any trouble," he said, "But they might want to talk to me." He had a hunch this fellow might be one of David's outposts. As wild and eccentric as he looked, there was a competency about him. "You might tell them Will Sigma's looking for them."

Punch glared at him and said, "You wait here or I'll put this next rock right in your left eye."

"I wouldn't want that to happen."

Sigma got off his horse and led him to a small trickle of water that flowed over what seemed to be solid rock. He tasted it himself and found it cold and clear—spring water. Sitting down . . . he waited and thirty minutes later—he looked up to see David stepping out from a crevice, followed by the tall sentry.

"Will!" he cried out. "What in the world are you doing here?"

"Looking for a free meal," he said.

"You've come to the right place. Come on."

Will shook the hand of David and then nodded. "Nice welcoming committee you've got here. Nearly hit my horse with that slingshot of his."

"He generally hits what he aims at. I saw him bring down a deer with that thing one time."

Punch looked at the Border Guard and sniffed. "How far will that shotgun of yours shoot? A hundred yards? A hundred feet?"

"About that, I guess."

"I'd have you out of the saddle before you got that thing unlimbered. Come on, let's go get something to eat."

Will laughed and clapped David on the shoulder. "Good to see you. We've got to talk some."

Will nodded and soon David led him through a wandering pathway through several canyons until he found a small valley, like a jewel, green and fresh.

"I never expected to see this."

"Punch knows all these places. Quite a few of them, if you know where to look. There's Starr." Starr came up and David said, "Look who's wandered in."

Starr came over at once and took Will's hand. "It's good to see you, Will," she said warmly. "I bet you're hungry, you always are."

"You know me, don't you."

"This is my brother, Josh and my sister, Miriam."

Will shook the boy's hand and then, when the young woman put out her hand, he took it, too. She was a beautiful girl, tall, willowy and shapely; Will was taken by her black hair and blue eyes. He grinned at David. "I don't believe she's any kin to an ugly thing like you," he said.

David laughed. "I've been told that before. Watch this one, Miriam. He's a real ladies' man."

Miriam liked the looks of Will Sigma. She made quick judgments and said, "Come along, Mr. Sigma, you can try your wiles out on me."

Will laughed and punched David on the arm. "Now, I don't

want to hear anymore from you. She knows a gentleman when she sees one."

Punch grunted, "She likes me; but of course I'm spoken for."

"Yes," Miriam said, winking at Will. "Too bad. All the good men are engaged. I suppose you are, too. Like Punch here."

"Not yet!"

"Well, good to have one eligible man in camp," Miriam smiled.

The group sat down and Miriam soon brought some fine stew and freshly-baked bread and put it before them. Will tasted it and smacked his lips. "I couldn't have done much better than this, myself."

"I could," Punch sniffed. "I just don't have time to do *everything*!"

The meal was pleasant. Under the blue sky with a soft breeze was blowing, David brought Will up-to-date on their journeys. Finally he said, "What's up, Will? You didn't come here by accident."

"No, I didn't. I saw Michael Kappa a few days ago."

"What's he up to?"

"Looking for you. Got a big bunch of Peacekeepers with him."

"We'd better move, hadn't we, David?" Miriam said.

"No need of that, Miss Miriam," Will Sigma said. "They're looking clear over on the other side of the Fields. I expect Michael will run their legs off before they try anything else. According to what he said, the Captain who's leading the bunch hasn't got sense enough to find his nose with both hands."

"It was nice of you to come and tell us," Miriam said.

She sat down across from Will and smiled at him. She had very white teeth and looking at her across the fire pleased Will. "I was glad to do all I can for you," he said. "But they'll be coming sooner or later," he added, glancing at David.

It was a pleasant time. Will found himself drawn more to David and Starr than ever. He'd always like them; but now it was Miriam who attracted him. He stayed two days and then decided, "I've got to go back. Maybe I'll find Michael and tell him where not to look."

"That would be fine. Thank you, Will," David said as he reached out to shake Will's hand.

Will asked hesitantly, "Your sister, how come she's never married?"

"Why, I don't know. She's only eighteen. You're not a candidate for her hand, are you? You'll have to come and ask my permission, you know."

Will was embarrassed. "I'm one of the 'roughs,' David. You know that. She'd never be interested in a fellow like me."

"If you had God in your life, she might be. She wouldn't be interested in any man unless he were a Christian."

Will Sigma looked down at the ground, then kicked a rock with the toe of his boot. As he looked up there was a lonesome quality in his gaze that was obvious to David. "I see men with families, wives, children . . . they've got everything." Then as if afraid he'd said too much, he turned and walked away.

Later David told this to Miriam who replied, "He is lonesome. I could sense it in him. But he's not one of us."

David gave her an odd look. He'd never seen his sister show such interest in a man. "Not yet," he said quietly. He smiled and said, "A smart girl like you might do something about that." He laughed, gave her a hug and turned and walked away.

After Sigma had gone, Miriam asked David about him several times. David concluded, "He's a good man, he just needs God." He put his arm around her and said, "Just like we all do, Sis. Just like we all do."

Chapter Seven

The Prophecy

The weather had turned cooler as the Remnant wandered through the Badlands. They discovered that, despite the rather terrible name, "Badlands," there were places in this country that were far from terrible. Punch, who seemed to know every inch of the territory, had led them to several oasises in the desert where the green grass and fresh water were as fine as anything they had seen. There were even strips of forest land. Not giant trees, to be sure, but the very sight of leaves and shade overhead had been refreshing to the wanderers.

One morning Punch approached David and looked up at the sky saying, "I think we'd better move from here."

David looked up quickly but saw nothing different in the signs of the sky and asked quickly, "Why? Do you think the Peacekeepers are coming this way?"

Punch scratched the bristle on his prominent chin and wiggled his shoulders expressively. "Well, I ain't no prophet," he said, "But somehow I get an itch right between my shoulder blades. It ain't never failed. Once it came to me when I was walking along in the middle of a desert. It came so strong. I jumped out of the way and a arrow whistled right by where I was!"

"Who was it, Punch?"

"Oh, just some old bandit. I stopped his clock, though." He

wiggled his shoulders again mumbling, "But I got that same feeling right now."

David stared at the apple-dried face of the guide and said, "I've been thinking about something. For some reason I've had Lazarus on my mind."

"Lazarus? Why, he's about past going, so I heard."

"Yes, he's not well. I want to see him once before he dies. He means a lot to me."

Punch pulled his crumpled hat from his head and ran his long fingers through his stringy hair. "Well, that wouldn't be too much of a trick. What we'll have to do is go around the big crater and take a short cut through Dead Man's Canyon. Then, if we cut through the big pass . . ." Punch went on for some time, tracing a route aloud, his bright eyes alert. David shook his head in wonderment as Punch concluded, "Well, you don't have to know all that, I reckon. What we'd better do is what we've been doing. Sleep by day and travel by night. Animals are in pretty good shape; so I think we can make it alright."

David quickly went to alert Starr and the others. They were all fairly well-rested now and Starr was glad to be going back to visit the old man.

"I've always felt like," Starr said as she threw some of her few belongings in a sack, "He knew more about my parents than he told us."

"He's been around a long time," David agreed. "I expect he's one of the last who actually remembers the old days."

Miriam had been putting her supplies into a sack of her own. She looked over at Starr and said, "It must be odd not to know anything about your family."

Starr pulled the mouth of the sack together and said, "Well, in the City they don't make too much of families."

"I can't imagine that," Miriam said. "A family was all we had. As I was growing up I felt so safe with a family around."

Starr straightened up and leaned against the rock wall that formed one side of the cave where they had found refuge. "I think that's why there's so much dissatisfaction and unrest in the City," she reasoned. "No one has anybody. I mean, the state takes on most of the responsibility of raising the children. So, you don't learn to love a state."

"I think that's right," David said. "There's something about having a father and mother, and brother and sisters, all tied together. It adds us to more than the sum of it."

"What do you mean, David? More than the sum of it?"

"Well," he struggled with his thoughts for a moment, then said slowly. "Everyone needs a place and everyone needs people, these two things are important. Our place was Haven. We knew everyone in the Village and most of the people in the next villages. It was our place, and no matter what happened in the City, we knew we were safe and secure."

"Or thought we were," Miriam said grimly. "It didn't turn out that way." The thought of the Gunships coming and blasting the Village to ruins brought pain to her eyes. Her lips drew into a thin line. "We lost our place and that was important to all of us."

David walked over and put his arm around Miriam. He loved his sister as he loved his brother. They had been a close family and he, no less than she, felt the pain of the loss of their parents and Tim. "We lost our place, but place isn't the most important thing. People are what's important. All through history people have been moved from one place to another. But as long as they held together, they were alright."

Starr, who had studied history most of her life said, "That's true. I was reading about one of the wars on earth. A country called Germany decided to get rid of all the Jews in their borders. It was interesting. I found a story of a Dutch woman called Corrie Ten Boom. She and her sister were yanked out of a nice, comfortable home, a good life and placed into a concentration camp. They lost all of their possessions, but they had each other. She said as long as she had her sister there with her, that was her place."

"What a nice way to put it," Miriam exclaimed. She looked up and saw Punch showing Josh how to shoot the ever-present slingshot. "I worry about Josh. He's so young to have his world torn up as ours has been."

"He'll be alright," David assured her. "We're all family. Not just us, but the whole Remnant. Brothers and Sisters. That's what's good about the Ecclesia, the elders take care of the widows and those who are hurting. Even those who don't have real families find one in the church."

Soon all their belongings were pulled together and piled into the wagon. The group pulled out just before dusk. Punch led them along a serpentine pathway around bogs and sinks and through blind canyons. When the moon arose, it shed its silver light down on them.

"It's almost as bright as day," David remarked to Punch as the two strolled along. He looked over at the tall, skinny guide and said, "You know every inch of this land, don't you, Punch?"

"I ought to. I've been over it all my life." He pointed ahead and said, "It'll take two days march, but we'll get to Lazarus' place soon enough." He was silent for a while and then remarked, "I don't understand what's going on, David. Why are the Peacekeepers after you and Starr so hot and heavy?"

As they strolled along, David explained that Starr had been one of the key personnel in the bureaucracy that held the City together. It was her job to keep people from finding out the truth. She was what was called a "Remedial Historian."

"What's that?" Punch asked.

"It means she went through the old books and removed all mention of God and the good things of the past. The City has evolved into a godless place. They can't afford to let people begin believing in Jesus. If they do, they'll lose control. That's why they want Starr back. They want her to make a public renunciation that she's no longer a Christian. That she was wrong to leave the City and its ways."

"Well, don't reckon she'll ever do that," Punch grinned. "She's pretty stubborn for a young woman."

"Yes, she is," David grinned ruefully, "Although I'd call it firm rather than stubborn."

The trip through the Badlands was broken by two nights rest. There was plenty to eat for game began to be abundant as the country grew more fruitful and verdant. Finally, they crested the mound of a low-lying bluff and Punch pointed down. "There it is!"

Starr came quickly to stand beside David and look down into the valley. It was on the very edge of the Badlands and had little of the arid look. The green trees were taller, although the leaves were beginning to change now to gold, red and yellow. They had arrived just at dawn as the morning sun picked up a glittering creek that wound its way in a snake-like fashion across the floor of the valley. Caught in one of the arms of the creek, almost held by it as if in an embrace, there sat a rather large cabin. A small spiral of smoke rose from the chimney and Starr said, "He's up! At least I hope it's Lazarus. I've been wanting to talk to him."

"Let's get down. We'll have to find a place for all these people to camp," David said. He led them down the slope which flattened out. They waded across the creek and, as usual, Joshua kept his eye out for likely-looking fishing spots. Then they reached the cabin David said, "Come on Starr. You and I will go in alone. We don't want to startle him by bringing this mob in on him."

"Alright, David."

The two of them walked across the meadow which was covered with attractive small plants. Starr reached over and plucked one. The flower had a greenish-white color. "What's this?" she asked.

David glanced at it and said, "We call it 'rattlesnake weed'."

"What an ugly name. Why do you call it that?"

"Well, some say it cures snakebites. Some people believe in it so strongly that they'll let a snake bite them for a price if you have these leaves on hand to apply to the wound."

Starr looked at the little flower and shook her head. "I don't think I'd want to try that. But it is good to see flowers again, isn't it?"

"Yes," David nodded. "Look at that one." He pointed to a tall plant. (Some of them were as high as six feet.) It had a dark purplish berry and large leaves. "That's polk weed," he said. "The old folks use it for rheumatism. They say it also makes a pretty good wine."

"I wish I knew flowers and plants like you do," Starr remarked. "I didn't learn anything but computers. I think flowers are better though."

They reached the door, which opened suddenly. Immediately they were confronted by an old man who was thin, almost to the point of boniness. His hair was long and uncombed and he kept it tied back with a small piece of string. When he held out his hands and the pair took them, they felt the fragility of the bones. It was almost like the bones of a small bird. His voice was cheerful though as he said, "David! And you Starr! Come in!" He looked over their shoulder and said, "It looks like you brought someone with you."

"Yes, Lazarus," David said. "You heard about Haven?"

A sadness came to the faded eyes of the old man and his head dropped for a moment. "I will miss your good father and mother and Timmy," he said. "I had many good friends in that place. But, come in."

The two walked inside and the old man suddenly swayed. He would have fallen but David reached him in time and eased him into a bed which was by one side of the wall.

Lazarus was breathing in short, stabbing breaths. His eyelids fluttered and he whispered, "Got to sleep, just a little bit—don't worry—I'll be alright."

David stared at him and saw that he indeed had dropped off into a fitful sleep. He leaned forward and stared at the face of the old man, then turned back to Starr. Shaking his head, he said, "He's not in good shape. He shouldn't be here by himself. I believe the Lord led us here to take care of him."

"We can do that," Starr said quickly. "You go take care of putting up camp. I'll fix him some stew or broth. He looks like he hasn't eaten in a long time."

David nodded, a worried look on his face, then turned and left the cabin. Going back to where the others were waiting, he said, "We'll camp over there under that grove. It's close to the water."

"How's the old man?" Punch asked.

"Not good, Punch. I don't think he's going to make it this time."

"Too bad. Won't be the same. Long as I lived I always knew Lazarus was here. Seems like he'd always show up when you most needed him. Always had a good word for us, even when there wasn't anything good happening."

Punch threw his energies into getting the tent set up. As soon as the camp was made, Josh asked, "Can we go hunting now?"

"I don't see why not." He looked up at the sky and remarked, "It ain't mid-day yet. Come along, maybe we can get something for the pot."

Punch left word with David that they were going out to hunt. Then, he and the boy left the camp. As they marched along, walking beside the creek, a fish flashed occasionally and Josh asked, "Can we come back and fish?"

"Well, we can't do everything today," Punch grinned, "But I reckon we can come out tonight and set out a few lines, if you like."

"I like it better than anything. I like to fish and hunt and be outdoors."

"Me, too, boy," Punch nodded with enthusiasm. "Never could stand to be tied down to work. Course there's some folks who don't like that, but that's just the way some of us are."

The two of them made their way to the low-rising hills that appeared in the west. Soon the horizon became a series of small peaks. The brush grew thicker and reached out to pull their clothing; but the two pressed on quickly. Punch halted, drew a deep breath and said, "That looks like a likely spot right there." He pointed to an open space around a small brook that wound around the mountainside.

"Why is it better than any other?" Josh asked curiously.

"Because the deer been here. See them tracks? I been followin'. They cleared out a place and sooner or later a good, fat, plump buck will come amblin' along and then we'll have our dinner." The two sat down and waited. Josh tried to talk a few times but Punch put a hand to his lips making a signal for silence. "You won't catch no deer babblin' like that," he scolded.

Josh flushed and settled down. He had his bow in his hand and kept the arrow notched, his left hand on the bow, his right loosely on the string. He had practiced for hours, getting expert instruction from the tall, skinny man beside him who seemed to handle any kind of weapon with ease. Punch carried a sword at his side along with a dagger, but only the ever-present slingshot in his belt. He pulled it out now, and placed a rock the size of a walnut beside it.

Josh had transferred some of the love for his father to this tall, ugly man who had such a kind heart. As he sat beside Punch he thought how misleading appearances can be. *Here's Punch,* he thought, *as ugly as a man can be; yet he's got a good heart. He'd do anything in the world for a fellow. I've known some people who looked good, but wouldn't give you the time of day.*

His thoughts were interrupted when suddenly two deer stepped out, a buck and a doe—both fat and plump.

Josh felt an elbow touch him, and when he cut his eyes around he saw Punch move his head slightly to the right and his lips form the word, "Mine!" By this Josh knew that Punch would take the doe with the slingshot and let him have the buck with the bow. His hands trembled for a moment, then Punch winked at him his sunken mouth turned up into a merry smile. When Punch nodded Josh knew he was telling him to take the first shot.

Slowly—very slowly, he lifted the bow, and an inch at a time drew it back until it was at his ear. The buck suddenly threw up his head and at once Josh launched the arrow. It flew through the air straight and true, then struck the buck in the side. The animal snorted and dashed out into the underbrush.

Josh was sick with disappointment when he saw that the walnut-sized rock had struck the doe in the head and she had fallen instantly and lay on the ground.

"We got 'em!" Punch yelled. "Come on!"

"Mine ran off," Josh said.

"He won't get far, not with that arrow in him," Punch said. "It was as good a shot as I've ever seen, Boy. You're going to be a fine hunter."

Punch's words proved true. They found the buck less than a hundred yards away, dead with an arrow near his heart. Punch carried him back and put him down beside the doe. "Well," he said, "We done good, but how we gonna get these animals back?"

"I know! I'll go get a pack animal."

"That's a good idea. You do that. I'll stay here and see that varmints don't get at 'em."

Josh made his way back to camp and, feeling very proud of himself, told David, "We got two deer. Enough food for all of us for a long time."

David clapped the boy on the shoulder. "Fine, I guess we'll have to depend on you to be the provider."

"Can I have a horse to take back to bring 'em in?"

"Of course. You're the hunter now, Boy. You'll have to take care of things like that."

That night they had a feast with fresh meat for everyone. There was singing as the sun went down behind the western mountains. David and Starr sat off to one side enjoying their food. When they had finished, they leaned back against a tree and listened to the singing. It was a hymn which said:

"Jesus is Lord."

"Jesus is Lord."

"He alone gives life and strength."

"Jesus is Lord of all the earth."

"I like that song," Starr said.

She leaned against him, his arm was around her. She felt safe as they sat there, close together, the warmth of his body coming through to her. Suddenly, with an impulse, she turned her face to him, reached up and pulled his head down. She kissed him tenderly. When she pulled back he asked her with surprise, "Well, what was that for?"

"It's just that—that I love you," she said simply.

His voice grew husky and he squeezed her tightly. "I'm glad of that, because I love you and I'd have to make you love me, if you didn't already."

She was serious however and said, "I've never had anybody, David. I've been alone all my life. It feels so good to have someone to love and to know that I'm not alone."

"We're all like that," he said. "Everyone needs someone."

"Yes, a place and a person," she said, remembering his words.

They sat for a while, then she remembered, "I need to go check on Lazarus."

"I'll go with you," he said. The two made their way past the group that was gathered around the fire and David saw that Josh was in the center of things. "Josh is going to be alright," he said. "When we lost our folks I was worried about him. He's lonesome for them, as I am, but he's alright."

They entered the cabin and found Miriam sitting beside Lazarus. "Is he alright? Has he awakened?"

"Not yet, David," she said.

She got up and David said, "Go get something to eat. We'll sit beside him."

"Alright." She hesitated and said, "He awoke up once and said something, but it was in a language I could not understand. It was like he was praying, I think, but I didn't know the words."

When she left the room, Starr sat down in the chair she had vacated and David pulled up another chair on the other side. They sat there silently watching the old man's lips tremble from time-to-time as if he were trying to speak. Finally, about an hour later, his eyes opened. He looked around the room calmly, his eyes pausing on Starr and then on David. He smiled and said, "It's time."

David leaned forward, patted the thin arm. "Are you hungry?"

"No, the next meal I eat will be at the Master's table."

Starr thought his mind was wandering but his eyes were clear. "The Master's table?" she questioned.

"Yes. The Lord Jesus said one time He would not drink wine again until he drank it new in the Kingdom; so the next meal I have will be with the King."

Starr knew at once that he meant the old man was dying and she asked, "Are you afraid?"

"Afraid?" Lazarus looked at her and surprise touched his weary eyes. "Why would I be afraid to go to Him who loves me more than anyone else? Every word in the New Testament is rustling with a breeze that says He loves us." He began to speak of the Lord Jesus. David and Starr listened, knowing that this would be his last night on earth. Finally he said, "You will find your parents. The Lord has told me that much. They are alive and you will be reunited with them."

"Oh, Lazarus!" Starr's eyes filled with tears. "Thank you, thank you!"

"You have been faithful to your Lord, my daughter," he said. "It has been hard for you. You have come out of great darkness. But God has a great blessing in store. He's going to do marvelous things through you. Be faithful to the Lord Jesus as He is always faithful to you.

He looked at David and said, "The world is going to go through a great darkness. There will be blood on the earth. There will be the cries of widows mourning and orphans, but this is not the end. Strong men like you must hold fast to the truth." He reached out his hands to either side, and when Starr and David took them, he held onto them for a time. Then, finally, he half-lifted himself up and gasped, "Praise God! He is always faithful, always faithful!" Then he slipped back and laid his head down. Ten minutes later, he ceased to breathe.

David and Starr folded his hands, the thin arms together on his chest and Starr reached out and arranged his hair on his forehead. Tears were in her eyes as she said, "He was such a good man."

David nodded, his own eyes not entirely dry, "Yes. A man of God and he has gone to meet the One he loved so much."

Chapter Eight

The Martyrs Of The Dome City

Leo Zeta was in charge of the roundup of undesirable aliens. It was not the first time the stubby hit-man had combed through the Dome City, searching for those who did not fit in with the city morals and codes. This was a job he enjoyed. Now, as he marched in front of a phalanx of white-garbed Peacekeepers, he stridently lifted his voice. "You have the names of those who have joined the Neo-Crossbearers. I want every one of them taken at once! They will *not* resist. They believe in peace and we intend to give it to them. A long eternal peace." His thick lips grinned fixedly as his hand sliced through the air with a powerful swiping blow as if it were a huge guillotine. "Take them all to the White Tower. They will be given a chance to recant."

Saul Lambda was standing nearby and, when he heard this, he said under his breath, "But none of them will. They never do."

He watched as Zeta handed out the orders to his Lieutenants and then moved to stand next to him. Leo said, "There must be no mistakes about this."

"Mistakes? I don't make mistakes, not when I'm doing my job!"

"See that you don't! Richard Xi's most serious about this. He demands that we root this group out."

"Won't be too difficult. They won't fight back. They never do. They're like a bunch of sheep."

"Strange you should say that," Lambda said thoughtfully. "Did you know that one of their symbols is a lamb?"

"A lamb? No, I never knew that."

"Yes. For some reason they find that to be satisfying. They even sing hymns about 'The Lamb of God'." He shook his head saying slowly. "I can't understand it. It's like a case of insanity that's become a plague. We stamp it out in one spot and then it breaks out in another. It's been going on for too long. It's got to stop."

Leo slapped his thick hand against his thigh and grinned broadly. "Don't worry, Saul. I'll take care of it."

The raids of the Peacekeepers were hardly worthy of the name. They hit every part of the Dome City with robot-like precision. First they went through the City offices and there took the names of those given to them. Some of the Lieutenants were surprised at the fact that several in high offices in the state were involved in the Neo-Crossbearers Union. But they did not resist arrest. Instead, they allowed themselves to be led away without so much as a single blow being struck.

In the Fringe, however, it was difficult. The people of the Fringe were more volatile and the Peacekeepers had more difficulty finding their victims. The streets wound around in a labyrinthine fashion, people lived in drain pipes, in shacks, some even on the street. There were many apartments hidden, as it were, behind shops or in the attics of the houses that ringed this district.

Leo Zeta moved along the street, his eyes searching. He caught a movement in a top window. "There!" he cried out. "Someone's up there! Go drag them down!"

His command was instantly obeyed. Soon two burly Peacekeepers appeared in the doorway, each of them holding onto the arm of a thin elderly woman who said not a word as she stared at her captors.

"Are you one of the Neo-Crossbearers?" Leo demanded.

The woman said without hesitation, "Yes, I believe in the Lord Jesus Christ."

Leo stared at her and even his rough manner seemed out of place. "There's no need for you to die, old woman," he said quietly. "Just tell me you won't have anything to do with these people and you can go."

A crowd had gathered to watch. The woman looked around at them, then smiled at Leo. "I can't do that, Sir. I must be faithful to my Lord."

"You can't be faithful to him if you're dead!" Leo snapped. It was a scene he had undergone several times before and, for some reason, it irritated him. Here was a woman who would soon be "relieved" of life anyway by the state, but he thought, *It looks like she'd cling to what little time she's got left. But, she's as crazy as the rest of them.* In a rough voice he announced, "Alright, take her to the Tower."

The woman turned to a tall man wearing plain clothing and said, "Good-bye, Son."

To Leo's surprise, the man nodded, saying sadly, "Good-bye, Mother. I'll be with you soon."

Leo stared at the man. "Are you one of the Neo-Crossbearers, too?"

"Yes," the man said firmly.

Leo was shaken. He had never seen people go so calmly to their certain doom. But his men were watching, so he had no choice. "Take him, too," he said. As the two were led down the street, the man holding his mother firmly, Leo gritted his teeth and said to one of his Lieutenants, "I don't understand these people. Don't they know they're going to be 'relieved'?"

"Of course, they know. They don't seem to care, do they? Makes you wonder."

"Wonder what?" Leo snapped.

"It makes you wonder if you could face death as calmly as they do."

"They're living in a fool's paradise; you know that." He gave the guard careful scrutiny. "You're not falling for this line about Heaven and living forever, are you?"

"Not me," the guard shrugged.

"That's good. Be sure you hang onto that thought."

Richard Xi stood before the captives. They had been gathered together, over three hundred of them in the largest room in the Tower. In this high ceiling room, white-clad guards stood holding their weapons firmly. Xi thought wryly, *That's rather unnecessary. Where would they run to?* But, he himself, had assigned the security for the White Tower and knew that they were only carrying out his orders. He glanced over to see Saul Lambda and Leo Zeta waiting for him. He mounted the small platform and looked out over the crowd—most of them dressed in rough clothing as was customary in the Fringe area. Xi announced loudly, "You know why you're here. You have proven yourselves to be disloyal to this City. You have all been given a chance to recant and you have refused. But I will give you one last chance. Turn away from this one you call Jesus and you will be free to go."

A silence fell over the crowd. There was a shuffling of feet, barely audible, and Xi watched eagerly, hopeful that at least some would avail themselves of this opportunity. But, no one moved and he became angry.

"You can die then! It will be a public execution. You will be an example to our loyal citizens." He nodded toward a tall, heavyset man wearing a black uniform. "Are your Relievers ready?"

"We are, Sir." There was a cold look in the eyes of the man dressed in black. He was an executioner, though his title was Chief Reliever.

He turned to the Peacekeepers and nodded, "Take them to the place of relieving."

What followed next was something that shook even those accustomed to those relieving people—relieving them of their lives.

The victims were taken to the largest square in the City. They were paraded before an audience of hundreds of people who had come to witness the execution. There was a holiday-air about the crowd. Richard Xi had seen that there was plenty of strong drinks so that there was a drunken atmosphere to the crowd.

"Let's see them go to meet their Lord," cried one drunk, who was barely able to stand up. "Give 'em what they want!"

The soon-to-be martyrs, who were lined up by groups of twenty, were assigned a Reliever. Some of the Relievers were men, some women. It was a job that Starr Omega had before her conversion.

"Have them sit down," the executioner commanded. Then all the groups were made to sit down in chairs. As the crowd grew more and more noisy, the executioner held up his hand. "Now, you may proceed."

Each group had a Reliever and a small table on wheels. On the table were hypodermic needles. Richard Xi watched the group nearest him. The Reliever approached the first victim, a strong man with long black hair. As customary, the Reliever said something to him, but the tall man merely shook his head. The Reliever took the hypodermic and plunged it into the man's arm, then removed it. Almost at once the man began to slump in his chair. If he had not been bound in it, he would have fallen. His head slumped forward and then he was still. Without a moment's wasted motion, the Reliever moved to the next chair which contained a young girl, no more than fourteen. Xi saw she was very pale. When the Reliever spoke to her, she also shook her head. As she looked to the woman on her right—Xi could read her lips. "Good-bye, Mother."

Although the woman could do no more than smile, there was

a look of victory on her face. Again Xi read her lips. "Not 'good-bye', for we will be with the King very soon."

Somehow the calmness of the three shook Richard Xi. They really believe that, he thought almost desperately. *They believe that as soon as they're dead they'll be with this King of theirs called Jesus.* He looked around at the crowd and saw some of those watching. Many were making fun of the victims. but others were impressed by the calmness with which the martyrs approached death.

On and on it went until Xi wanted to leave. It was an efficient-enough matter. The Relievers moving from person to person, each with their own small group. Finally, the executioner turned to him and said, "Your orders have been carried out, Sir."

"Let them remain on public display for the rest of the day before they are diminished," Xi said. He turned and hurried away. When he was in his office, he opened his liquor cabinet, pulled out a bottle and poured a glass half full. He drank it all, then shuttered and took another. The execution had troubled him more than he wanted to admit. A knock at the door startled him and quickly he moved to replace the bottle and glass. Returning to his desk, he said, "Come in."

Leo Zeta and Saul Lambda entered, both of them smiling. "Well," Lambda said, "That was quite impressive."

"Yes, that'll teach 'em a lesson," Leo agreed.

Richard Xi stared at the two men and thought, *What fools they are. Didn't they see that many in that crowd were impressed by the way those people died? They'll be wanting the same thing. Whatever it is that gave them their courage. They're desperate for it.* Then Xi said, "Very well, but we're not through yet."

"You're right about that," Lambda said. "We haven't even scratched the surface."

"What about those down in the Shadowland? It seems that place is crawling with Neo-Crossbearers."

"They'll have to be rooted out," Xi said almost angrily.

"We'll take care of it," Lambda said, nodding with assurance. "Don't worry about it, Richard. We're going to whip this thing."

But Richard Xi quickly discovered that it was one thing to execute people, but their execution brought on other problems. In the next few days he received report-after-report of those who had fled to the Shadowland to escape. And, he knew that this was a different sort of problem. He pondered over the solution for days and almost at once put his finger on one difficulty.

"So many people," he said to his assistant, a woman named Sylvia, "Are leaving the City. We're going to have trouble."

"Let them go," Sylvia shrugged. She was a tall woman with brassy hair and hard gray eyes. "We can always find them and execute them."

Xi stared at her. "You don't understand," he said in a withering tone. "These are the people who work. They keep this City running. They're the manuals. Are you going to get out and clean the streets when we kill all the manuals off?"

Sylvia saw her mistake at once. She swallowed and shook her head. "I didn't understand that. Of course, we can't have such a thing."

"It creates difficulties. We actually don't know too much about what goes on down in the Shadowland. But I know there's a hotbed of heresy. Our spies have told us that much at least."

"Why not just let them stay down there as long as they're not making any noise about this Christ of theirs. What harm can they do?"

Drumming his fingers on the desk, Richard Xi thought about this. It was not the first time it had occurred to him. "We can't do it," he said finally.

"Why not, Sir?"

"Because you can't contain the thing. We can't kill all the Neo-Crossbearers or the City will shut down. Same thing's true in the Fields. Who'd grow the grain to make our fuel if we kill everyone out there? We've got to learn to control them and there's only one way to do it."

"What is that, Sir?"

Richard Xi stared at her saying, "We'll enslave them. That's the only answer. They'll either get rid of this Christ of their's or become slaves!" He leaned back and said almost nervously, "That ought to do it. If it doesn't . . ." He hesitated, then realized Sylvia was staring at him strangely. "But it will, of course. We'll see to it."

Chapter Nine

A Last Resort

Leo Zeta had returned to his unit in the Badlands. He needed more reinforcements and the recent execution of the Neo-Crossbearers had made him more determined than ever to root out such heresy in the Fields.

"I've got to find this woman," he told Michael Kappa. The two were standing in the middle of some of the most-arid-looking land one could ever see. They had been traveling for six days now and had encountered nothing but those in scabby villages scattered over the countryside and a few sheep herders and pig keepers.

"It's gonna be hard to find them. This is a big country," Michael replied.

"I thought you knew it."

"I'm not sure any of us know it very well." He cast his eyes around the barren landscape saying, "Who'd want to come and spend time here?"

In exasperation, Zeta said, "We've got to keep on. We must move faster."

"We'll kill the horses if we do," Kappa remarked. He was honed thin by the sun and the difficult travel but his eyes were still hard and tough. "Which direction shall we go?"

The question brought Zeta no comfort. He half-turned, looking around over the landscape. The view was the same—piles of broken rock, miles of nothing but sand, with only a few water holes that were almost impossible to find.

"You're supposed to be the guide!"

"Too much for me," Kappa groaned. He hesitated, then said, "Will Sigma, one of the Border Guards, spent most of his life in here."

"He knows this country?"

"Pretty well. Better than anyone else,"

"Well, fetch him. How long will it take?"

" I think I can bring him back by tomorrow."

"Do it then. And hurry!"

Kappa left the camp that night and the next morning appeared in front of Zeta's tent. "This is Will Sigma, Captain."

Zeta stared at the man beside Kappa. He was tall and the wind blew his sandy hair awry. He didn't look like much, clad almost in rags; but there was a cool exterior about him. He kept his shotgun constantly in his hand. "He looks tough enough," Zeta whispered. Aloud he said, "Can you find this woman for us?"

"I can look and you can go along, Captain."

The answer was spare, but it was all that Zeta had. "alright. We'll pull out at once."

"Better take all the water you can haul," Will Sigma instructed. "It gets a little scarce in some places."

The troop pulled out at once—the horses bearing all the bags of water that they could carry. For the next three days, Leo Zeta had the worst time of his life. The horses grew footsore, and when the water holes turned out to be dry, they quickly exhausted their small stock. Finally, Zeta knew that the search was hopeless. It bothered him to do it, but he opened up the channel on his radio and sent a message. He knew it would create anger and perhaps get him into trouble, but he had no other choice. Late that afternoon the Gunships appeared. Zeta watched grimly as his men staggered on board, almost dead from dehydration and fatigue. He glared at Will Sigma saying, "Don't expect any pay for what you've done. You didn't do anything."

Sigma did not answer—not even a smile. Then Michael Kappa asked, "Do you want me to go back with you?"

"No! You two stay out here. Cover all the ground you can. Others will come. We've got to find that woman!"

Sigma and Kappa watched as the last of the guards boarded. The last man on was Leo Zeta, and he pulled the door shut with a clang. The giant copters began to rise, until soon they were nothing but dots in the sky—and then they were gone.

Kappa grinned at Will. "Not much of a guide, are you?"

"Not much," Will shrugged. A touch of humor came to his eyes and he said, "A couple of times we almost blundered into water holes. I didn't want that to happen."

Kappa looked at the horizon saying, "You think they'll be back?"

"You know they will! From what I hear, Richard Xi's about to go crazy. He'd kill everyone in the Fields if he didn't need them."

"Suppose we go over and have a talk with David and Starr," Kappa suggested. "Then I can report back that I can't find them."

"Alright. Let's go."

Richard Xi was furious. He stared at Leo Zeta and Saul Lambda saying, "You realize what this failure means? Sooner or later we're going to pay for it and I think it'll be sooner."

Zeta said defensively, "I couldn't help it, Sir. That land out there's too big, and there's a thousand holes those rats can run into."

Lambda asked, "What if we send out all the Gunships?"

"I don't think it'd make any difference," Zeta shrugged. "As soon as they hear the sounds of the rotors they hide. I think they stay out all night and hide in the day time. If you'd just let me kill some captives off . . ."

But the memory of the execution of the martyrs was too firmly fixed in the mind of Richard Xi. "No! No!" he said quickly. "That just encourages the others. As I've told you, we can't kill them all. But we've got to do something!"

The three men talked for a long time. One would come up with a suggestion that would be immediately scoffed at by the others. In truth, none of them had any experience in this sort of thing and they were all somewhat desperate. Their desperation made them snappy, until Zeta came up with a possible solution.

"Maybe we've been going about this all wrong," he said almost in a whisper.

"What other way is there?" Xi snapped.

"Well, there might be another method."

Lambda exclaimed, "If you've got any ideas, Leo, spit it out! We've got to do something!"

"Well, it's just an idea." He stroked his thick jowls with one hand, scratching at the whiskers he had not bothered to shave off. "Obviously, we can't get at 'em by sending the Gunships in. Agreed?"

"Yes, yes, we've already said that," Xi said. "What's your idea?"

"My idea is to send someone in who can find them and then radio in their location. That way we'll have them pinned down."

"Are you volunteering for the job?"

"No, not me." A touch of fright came to Zeta. He remembered the burning desert and the bones of those who'd lost their way. He was not a timid man, but something about the stillness of that place intimidated him.

"What then? Ask one of the Border Guards."

"That might be alright," Lambda said. "But some of them don't know the place any better than you do. They only know the Fringe."

"That's right," Leo said. He leaned forward and his eyes gleamed. "But, there's a man who knows it. I don't know if he'll take the job, though."

"Who is it?" Xi demanded.

"Mingo."

At the sound of the name, Saul Lambda laughed hoarsely. He shook his head in disgust. "Is that the best you can come up with?"

Xi was interested. "Who is this Mingo?"

"Nothing but a traitor," Lambda said. "I don't know why we haven't executed him already."

Leo Zeta admitted, "He's a traitor alright, and a dangerous man. But he knows that desert out there like the back of his hand. I think he must have been born in the Badlands, if I remember correctly. He knows every rock and water hole in the place."

"Where is he?" Xi asked.

"Right here in the White Tower."

"We've been trying to re-program him. He'd be a valuable man if he'd just show some judgment."

Xi stared at the two men. "You think he could find Omega?"

"I *know* he could," Leo said, "But the question is, *will* he."

"We can make it worth his while," Xi said. "We can give him a pardon and all the credits he needs. He can't turn it down."

"You don't know Mingo," Zeta shook his head. "I've seen tough ones before, but none like him."

"Still," Lambda said, stroking his hair nervously, "He's been in isolation for a long time. If I know the man, he's dying for the sight of trees and the open sky."

"Let's have him in," Xi said. "All he can say is no. But I think we can make our offer pretty attractive."

"Come on, Mingo. You've got an appointment."

The man lying on the pad rose. His motion was like a cat. The cell itself was only eight feet square. There were no windows and only a single door. There were no pictures on the wall, no books, no television—nothing—just four bare walls, a ceiling and a floor. Although no more than five-feet ten inches, there was a strength about him that most men lacked. He had a thatch of thick auburn hair, bright blue eyes, and a wedge-shaped face. With his wide forehead and a chin that had a pugnacious tilt to it, Mingo stared at the guard and said nothing. This irritated the guard, who liked his prisoners to plead. Mingo had not said one word to him in all the time that he had been confined.

"Come on! I hope they hang you."

Mingo merely looked at the guard, shrugged his shoulders and followed him out. As they walked down the corridor, Mingo stretched, seeming to enjoy the space after the confines of the cubicle. His eyes moved about as if he were outside looking for signs of life in a forest or a desert. He was one who was not made for life inside, but for the outdoors. His face now pale from the long confinement, there was nothing but an adamant set to his chin as he moved down the corridors.

When they reached a door the guard nodded at the two attendants, one of whom commanded, "Go on in."

The door opened and the guard shoved Mingo inside slamming the door behind him.

Mingo paused and looked quickly around the room. He knew one of the men and said quietly, "Well, hello Leo. Haven't seen you in a while."

Leo's eyes gleamed with anger, but he was on his best behavior."

"Hello, Mingo. Glad to see you again. This is Saul Lambda and I believe you've heard of Richard Xi, in charge of the White Tower."

Xi responded, "Have a seat, Mingo."

"If you don't mind, I'd rather stand. I've done a lot of sitting lately."

"As you will." Xi was impressed by the steady gaze of the blue eyes. He studied the man while trying to figure what was on the inside. But it was as if Mingo had a wall about him. "There's no give to this man," he said. "He'll do what he wants to do, or die."

Xi was a good psychologist. He knew that there was no point in trying to warm up to this man, to make him feel comfortable. He said immediately, "There is something we need from you."

"Oh? What is that?"

"We need someone to go to the Badlands, out in the Fields, and find an escaped criminal."

Mingo glanced over and said, "What's wrong with you, Leo?" When there was no answer and Leo Zeta flushed, Mingo grinned slightly. "You couldn't find 'em, eh?"

Xi saw Zeta's face flush with anger and said, "I'll be truthful with you, Mingo. We've tried our best and we can't find this fugitive. I'd like to have you try it. Do you think you could find them?"

"Don't know."

"Would you be willing to try?"

Mingo looked over at the other two men. "I understand there are some charges against me. Zeta told me the last time I saw him that I'd rot in my cell."

"Things change," Richard Xi said smoothly. "We're willing to pay well for your services.

"Not interested."

Xi was shaken by the instant refusal. "You couldn't like it down in that cell. You're a man of the outdoors. Even I can see that. If you find this criminal for us, I'll see that you get a free pardon. You might have to leave the City, but that wouldn't bother you, would it?"

"You can't pardon him, Sir." Argued Saul "He's a heretic. He's against everything we stand for!"

Xi threw a sharp glance at him. "Be quiet, Saul!" He turned

his eyes again to Mingo and said quietly. "I know you're not a man who bargains. Neither am I. I'll make you one offer. If you say no, that's final. Back to your cell. We'll find another way."

"What if I say yes?"

A slight smile touched the lips of Richard Xi. "I think I know you, Mingo. You're not interested in credits or rising to the top here in the City. But I know something you do want."

Mingo regarded the man cautiously. He recognized the strength of Richard Xi, realizing that he was a smarter man than either Lambda or Zeta. Xi's eyes seemed to plunge into Mingo. "What do I want?" he asked softly.

Xi leaned forward on his desk, clasping his hands. His voice was almost soft as a summer's breeze. "You want to be out in the green Fields. You want to see the blue sky over your head. You want to walk beside rivers and streams, swim in the lakes. You want to be your own man, out there."

Mingo stared at the small figure, their eyes locked. "That's right," he said.

"It's yours. All you have to do is find one person. Then you're free. All charges against you will be dropped. You can't live in the City, you understand."

There was silence in the room as the three men watched Mingo. There was nothing to be revealed in his eyes or on his features. The silence ran on so that it became almost unbearable. Then, Mingo suddenly nodded sharply. "alright, I'll do it. But, that's all I'll do, and once I'm out there, don't send anyone to get me. That would be 'expensive'."

"Agreed!" said Xi. He stood to his feet, "The person we want is a woman named Starr Omega. We know she's in the Badlands but apparently she has good guides. Go bring her in."

"That might be hard to do. I'm not sure you can handle it," Zeta said.

"You got a picture of her?" Mingo asked.

"Give him what he needs," Xi said. He looked toward Mingo and said, "I have the feeling I won't see you again. When you find the woman, turn her over to us, then you're free to do as you please. But, I'd advise you to stay clear of the Neo-Crossbearers."

A flicker of interest sparkled in the blue eyes of Mingo. "Why is that?"

"Because. They're not going to last long," Xi said bluntly. "That's the charge against this woman. She's joined them, which unless she recants, is likely to be fatal for her."

"I've heard a little about the Neo-Crossbearers," Mingo said. "Not likely that they would have a fellow like me. But, I'll bring her in. Then, we're quits!"

Xi nodded again. "Give him whatever equipment he needs, as much help as he needs. Mingo, all of our forces are at your disposal. We found out, however, it doesn't do any good to send Gunships in. You'll have to find her alone. There might be some pretty tough men protecting her."

The information registered on Mingo but he said nothing. Then Xi said, "Good-bye and good hunting!"

Chapter Ten

The Raid

Leo Zeta felt insecure about sending the man called Mingo out on a mission. Zeta was an organization man. He did not trust anyone outside the system in which he himself functioned. Now, as they approached the river that separated the Fringe from the Fields, he was sure a mistake had been made.

"What's your plan?" he demanded, as they halted at the river's edge.

Mingo looked up, his wedge-shaped face impossible to read, "My plan is to do whatever I have to to stay out of the White Tower."

"I know that!" Zeta exclaimed." However, I need to know your movements."

Mingo stepped up to the sleek horse that he had chosen from the stables. With one smooth movement, he stepped into the saddle and picked up the lines. "I'll write you a letter," he said. "Of course, the postal service is a little slow from the Badlands."

"I don't need any of your insolence."

"Then I won't give you any." Mingo looked out across the Fields that were half hidden by the early morning mist. The sun was barely clearing the rim of the horizon and Mingo was anxious to be on his way. "I'll get the girl, deliver her, and then we're quits. That's all you need to know." Touching the stallion with his heels, he quickly rode away.

With face flushed with anger, Zeta called out to Mingo, "You'll get the girl—and then I'll see that you get yours, Mingo!" He turned and trudged back toward the City. His thoughts were filled with revenge and mixed with ambitious plans and schemes to rise to his proper niche in the City.

Mingo rode steadily into the Grasslands, taking deep breaths of air and drinking in the scenery. The white confinement in the cell had taken its toll on him. He had thought he would go mad after a few days in that place and perhaps he did. He had batted his head against the sides of the walls, hoping to kill himself. But the Guardians had foreseen that and the walls were made of soft, padded leather so that all he could do was give himself a headache.

"I'm not going back to that place, Boy," he muttered fondly slapping the water-smooth silver stallion on the shoulder. He named the horse Silver and knew that they were going to be great friends.

The horse shook his head and was lifted into a pert gallop. He too was glad to be out of the City, for the big horse loved to run. When the man felt this he said, "Alright, let's go!" Silver opened up into a full dead run and Mingo leaned forward, laughing aloud as they tore along the well-marked trail that led into the Fields.

Mingo finally pulled the reins of the big horse, then allowed him to pick his way along at a fast walk. He thought about how he had defeated the system in his cell. He had learned how to blank his mind out so that hour-after-hour and day-after-day he would sit thinking nothing of the present, but going back and reliving his childhood. He had been amazed at how much he could remember and how the hours had passed once he learned this technique. Still, it had been a bitter pill being locked away from the sky and the earth that he loved. He had spent many years in the Fields, staying as far away from the City as possible and now, going back made the blood run faster through his veins.

He rode all morning, pausing at noon for a small meal that he had brought in his saddlebags. He loosed the saddle on the big horse and let him drink at the small stream while he sat there listening to the murmur of the water as it bubbled over the smooth rocks. The water was so clear that he could see the tiny flashing form of minnows that darted about. The minnows stayed together in groups and he wondered, not for the first time, how they knew to swim together. "Better than any troops," he murmured aloud, watching the flashing forms. At that moment, a large fish suddenly appeared, breaking water, turning it into white froth.

"I'd like to get you in a skillet," Mingo grinned. The thought intrigued him and he reached into his saddlebags for a line that he had packed as part of his equipment. He had known that he would have to furnish his own food. Now here he was, fishing in the clear stream with a sapling for a fishing pole. Almost at once he got a strike and he cried out, "Gotcha!" as he caught the fish that struggled vainly to escape. He drew the silvery form out and admired him saying, "Must be at least three pounds."

Despite the fact he had just eaten some cold meat, he broke out his camping gear, made a fire then fried the fish there beside the creek. When he had finished, he picked at it with his knife, the white flesh falling away in tender chunks. He added a little salt and sat there enjoying the first good food he had had in months. *This is the way to live!* he thought. *I'll never go back to that place again.*

Mingo rose, saddled Silver and rode off into the Fields. That night he camped in the elbow of a small creek, catching another fish and being lulled to sleep by the murmuring of the waters. It was cold, and using his saddlebag for a pillow, he wrapped himself up in his blanket. Overhead the stars dotted the sky like tiny flakes of fire. *They look like fireflies, except they're a little larger,* he thought. *A fellow would never get those counted. There must be millions of 'em!* He watched the stars for a while and saw a shooting star draw a silver streak against the ebony blackness of the sky.

"Someone said you make a wish when you see that," he said. "I wish I could get back to the Fields and never go anywhere close to the Dome City again." He realized he was bitter over his arrest and captivity and knew that he would never allow himself to be taken. *I'll get the girl,* he thought just as he dropped off to sleep, *And they can have her. Then, I'm quits with all of 'em.*

For three days he rode through the country. He met a few herdsmen, stopped to talk to farmers, never giving any hint of his mission. Finally, he came to a village that he knew and made his way down a familiar street. A hovel with a thatched roof was his target. He slipped off his stallion, tied him carefully, then marched over and knocked on the door. "Abbadon!" he called out.

"Who is it?"

"Mingo."

A silence followed his words and then a rustling came from inside the room. The door creaked open and a bleary eye peered out at him. "Can't be you," a hoarse voice grunted. Then the door opened and a man stepped outside. He was dirty and his face was twisted with what seemed to be a continual rage. "It is you," he muttered. "How'd you get out?"

"Glad that you got such a good welcome for me, Abbadon," Mingo nodded. "I've got a job for you."

"What kind of job?"

"Not much of one," Mingo shrugged. "You want it or not?"

"I'm pretty busy. I'd have to be well-paid."

Mingo laughed sharply. "I can see you're jammed up with people wanting to hire you." He pulled some gold from his pocket and let it clink in his fingers. Gold was unknown pretty much in the City, but some of it circulated in the Fields. It could be traded for almost anything.

Abbadon's eyes brightened when he saw the gold coins. "What's the job?" he said.

"I've got to capture a fugitive who is hiding somewhere in the Fields, maybe in the Badlands. You know that country as well as any."

"Who is it?"

"A woman. Her name is Starr Omega. The fellow with her is named David."

Abbadon's face twisted into a snarl. "Those two, eh?"

"You know them?"

"I know them." Abbadon did not reveal the fact that David had once beaten him half-to-death for attempting to molest Starr Omega when she first came to the Fields. Abbadon had burned with revenge ever since. Now he grunted, "They're being hunted all over the place now, Gunships everywhere."

"So I heard. Are you ready to go?"

It was not much of a chore for Abbadon to pull himself together. He had a horse that he mistreated badly and the animal's eyes began to roll as he settled down on his back. He looked around saying, "Are we going to meet the Peacekeepers?"

"Naw, no Peacekeepers. Just you and me."

Abbadon stared at him. "David's a pretty rough fellow. We may need some help."

"Oh, I think we can handle it," Mingo replied. "I've been gone a while. We got to go pick up some word of 'em. Maybe some of your friends will know; that is if you have any."

Abbadon shot him a hard look. "They'll have to be paid, too!"

"We'll pay for information, but it'll have to be good. Come on. I've got a few ideas myself."

The search for the Remnant proved to be more difficult than Mingo thought. For one thing, it wasn't easy to pick up information. David had many friends and none of the farmers that they encountered seemed inclined to give information, if indeed they had any. For over a week Mingo and Abbadon rode many miles, searching for a clue—some hint of where the small group might have gone. Then one night over the campfire Mingo said, "We'll go to the village Zeta left. According to him, he was getting close. But, you never know."

"There are a couple of Border Guards who know this country pretty well. If we could find either one of them, they might help."

"Who are they?"

"One of them is Michael Kappa and the other is Will Sigma."

"Yes, Zeta told me about them. They didn't seem to help much, though."

The next morning the two rode out early and stayed in the saddle until they reached the small village where Zeta had been forced to abandon the search. Their luck seemed to change when Abbadon came back from one of his rides saying excitedly, "I found out something!"

"What is it?" Mingo demanded.

"A man named Asaad—I wouldn't trust him with anything, but he knows a lot about what goes on out here."

"What did he say?"

"He claims that the Remnant left here and went over there past the dunes—out in the Badland country."

"That's a big country. We could wander around just like the Peacekeepers did."

"Asaad says he knows exactly where they are. Says one of the herdsmen out there, his kinsman, saw them. They got a camp near some caves. We'll never find it unless we have a map."

"Let's go see Asaad."

The two rode quickly toward the village. They found Asaad, a small man with penetrating eyes, seated at a table—his back to the wall—in a small gloomy tavern.

"Alright. Here's your man," Abbadon said. "Now, let's have the map."

Asaad shook his head abruptly, "Not so fast," he whispered. "There's a little matter of cash first."

"What's your price?" Mingo demanded. He waited until the small, dirty figure named an amount and then laughed. "I didn't come to buy the Fields," he said. "We'll find them, but if you want to sell your information, you'll have to be reasonable."

A time of bargaining went on until an agreement was made. Mingo counted out ten gold coins, handed them over, whereupon Asaad reached into a recess of his dirty garment and pulled out a single roll of paper. Mingo unrolled it, laid it on the table and stared at it. "I know this place," he said. He put his finger on the small "x" asking, "Right here?"

"That's what the herdsman said."

"They may have moved by now," Abbadon complained. David's pretty smart.

"I don't think so," Asaad said shaking his head. "There's plenty of water there and lots of game."

Smiling Mingo said, "We'll go take a look. If they're not there I'll expect a refund or better information." He rose and left the room, Abbadon following right behind.

They mounted their horses and rode out of the dusty village. "I think the search party should be larger. There's more than just David out there."

"The larger the search party, the easier they'll be able to see us coming. This is a job that takes silence. We'll stalk them. If you don't want in on it, give the coins back and we'll call it quits."

But Abbadon shook his head. "No, I've got a score to settle with David. Were your orders to bring him back?"

"They want the woman. Didn't say anything about David."

"I'll take care of him myself. It will be easier to travel with just the woman to watch over—that is, after we get out of there."

"Nothing happens to the woman. You understand that?" Mingo

said sharply. Abbadon nodded his head. Mingo touched his heels to Silver's flanks. "Let's go. I want to get this over."

It was almost dusk when Starr came out of the cave. She had a water pot in one hand as she moved down the slope to where the spring bubbled out of what seemed like solid rock. She shivered a little noticing that the air was growing chilly. The smell of cooking meat was in the air as she scanned the horizon looking for the sign of riders.

"I wish David would come back," she said aloud. She smiled at her own voice and thought, *A woman in love does silly things. Talking to yourself is one of them, I guess.*

Starr moved on down the slope, following the trail which zigzagged through the rocks. She finally came to a small room-like crevice in the sheer walls. Somehow the water from above had eaten into the softer rock beneath and sought its level. Now it bubbled over, almost making a pleasant sound as it started its journey down the mountainside. Starr stooped and sunk the pot into the cold water. When it was filled she tugged it up, grunting at the weight of it. She sat the pot to one side. Then stooped down and leaned over, holding her hair back to keep it from falling into the water. The water was so cold it hurt her teeth. But it was delicious. Better than anything she'd ever had in the City!

She straightened up and was about to pick up the pot when suddenly hands seized her. She started to scream, but a strong hand was clapped over her mouth. She struggled with all her might, but was like a child in the hands of the strong arms that held her.

"I've got her. Go get the horses ready."

"What about the man?" A dark figure emerged from the corner. Fear raced through her heart as she recognized this evil man—Abbadon. He grinned at her and said, "We meet again, Starr Omega."

"Never mind that, get the horses!"

The two had waited for two days for an opportunity to find Starr alone. They had hidden out in the rock, keeping the horses well back so that they could not be heard. They had crept from stone-to-stone and kept surveillance of the Remnant. Now Starr had been identified by Abbadon as they had waited their chance.

"Don't struggle. I'm not going to hurt you." Mingo kept his hand over the woman's mouth. He picked her up bodily and carried her away. As soon as they were a hundred yards away, he put her feet on the ground and said, "Now, you can do this two ways. I'll either gag you and you might strangle, or you can give me your word that you won't cry out. Will you give me your word?"

Starr looked at the man who had captured her. Fear raced through her as she identified him as one from the City. She nodded and at once he released his hand.

"That's smart," he said. "Now, come along." He kept his hand firmly on her arm. His grip was so strong that she knew she could never break away. The two stumbled over broken rocks and stones as darkness was quickly falling.

"Where are you taking me?" Starr gasped.

"Back to the City."

Starr's heart sank as fear rose up in her. "Please," she begged, "Don't take me back there."

Mingo turned to look at the woman. He had not thought of her as a person—merely as his ticket to getting out of prison. Now, as he saw her large eyes and attractive face in the fading light, something came to him. He disliked this job, but there was no other choice.

"There's no sense talking about that," he grunted. "Come along."

Ten minutes later they arrived at the point were Abbadon stood with the horses. They had picked up two more horses so Starr was quickly tied to the saddle of one of them. Mingo took the long lead rope from the horse Starr sat on and said, "Come on." He got into the saddle and the three of them rode out at once.

The stars were bright in the sky and the moon made a huge silver disc. It was a beautiful evening, cool with the first promise of winter, maybe even snow in the air.

But Starr Omega was not thinking of the beauty of the night. She was thinking, *I've lost it all. I'll never see the Fields again.*

Chapter Eleven

A Whisper In The Night

When David rode back out to the camp, he felt an unexpected surge of well being. This place, hidden in the Badlands, an oasis, had become home for him. A tiny spiral of smoke went up and he reminded himself that it was such a sign as this that might give them away. But they had to cook and have fire. He had been out on a sweep of the area for two days and had been pleased to find no signs of pursuit whatever. Slipping off his horse, he stripped off the saddle and bridle, and turned the animal out in the corral, still containing enough grass for a hungry horse. Slapping the horse on the back he said, "There you are, Boy. You've earned your keep." He watched as the animal bent and began to chomp hungrily at the short, dried grass. David muttered, "We'll have to go get some feed for the horses. That grass won't last long." He straightened his shoulders, picked up his saddlebags and walked along the path toward the camp. It was a wild rugged place, but water was available and there were trees which served as a shelter. He crossed over into the last perimeter and was at once accosted, "Halt! Stop! Halt! Stay where you are!"

David grinned, saying, "That you, Punch?"

Punch came out from behind a cluster of small trees, the ever present slingshot held firmly in his left hand, the right holding the rock. He grinned at David as he put the slingshot up saying, "You'd better sing out. I nearly put your lights out before I saw who you were."

David shook his head. "Any sign of trouble around here?" When Punch didn't answer, David looked up in surprise. He stopped before the tall man and saw something that disturbed him. "What's the matter?" he demanded quickly.

"Well—it's not good news."

"What is it? Has there been another attack?"

Punch pulled off his hat, scratched his scruffy hair. "You might say that," he grunted. "Starr's gone."

The unexpected news sent a shock through David. "What do you mean—gone?" he demanded.

"I mean, she's gone. She went out last night to get water from the spring and never came back."

David stared at the face of Punch and tried to get it all straight. "Did you go after her?"

"Well sure we went after her but it was dark. We couldn't follow signs in the dark. But this morning," Punch said in defense, "I saw some signs of trouble down by the spring. Someone grabbed her, looks like, and carried her off. They had horses, too, four of them. They went off that way."

"Why didn't you go after her?"

"Because I can't track over solid rock. That's why. I guess they knew that," Punch said angrily. "Who do you think it might be? There are no bandits out here. They would have jumped us for money, not just taken her."

David thought quickly. "I think someone in the City got smart. They knew that Gunships couldn't sneak up on us so they sent a raiding party out. I'm going after her."

"I'll get a bunch together."

"No. A bunch is no good. We'll have to find them and ambush

them. If they saw us coming they might kill Starr or keep her for a hostage."

"Well, I'm going and that's flat." Punch was angry at what happened and felt he was partly to blame. "You'll need a fresh horse. He's all ready. I thought you might be back. You better eat something."

David shook his head stubbornly. "No, we don't have a minute to lose. I'll go up and say good-bye to Miriam and Josh. You get the horses and load plenty of supplies. We don't know how long this chase will take."

"Alright. I'll be ready when you get back."

David moved on toward the cave that served as the main dwelling-place. He was greeted by several, but when they saw the set of his jaw they offered no light talk.

"David!" Miriam ran to him as soon as he entered with Josh right behind her. "They took Starr!"

"I know," David said grimly. "Punch and I are going after her."

"Take me too David," Josh pleaded.

"I'd like to but this is going to be a hard hunt."

Josh begged, "Please, I've got to learn how to be a man sometime."

David looked at the tall, lanky boy and thought of his own childhood. He had once been left at home from a hunt by his father. After all these years, the hurt of it was still there. He looked over at Miriam and saw the fear in her eyes. "alright." David said, "Get ready. We're leaving right away. Go down and tell Punch to get another horse for you."

Josh dashed out the door. Miriam argued, "It'll be too dangerous, David. Leave him here."

"He's got to learn somehow. I know he's young, but I'll look out for him."

"And who'll look out for you?" Miriam asked. "Those men are probably killers. They wouldn't send anybody else, would they?"

"No, probably not." Answered David, his heart as heavy as he could ever remember. "I didn't realize how much I loved Starr until this happened. We should never take our happiness for granted, Miriam. We ought to live every day as if it were our last."

"I know." Miriam came over and put her hand on his arm. "But you'll bring her back. I know you will. God wouldn't let this happen."

David felt a moment's despondency. His face usually so cheerful grew solemn as he shook his head, "I don't know—we don't know what God has in store for us. Sometimes bad things happen to good people. Look at our parents."

"I know," Miriam said. "I know that, but we can pray. The Bible says that He wants to give us the desires of our hearts, doesn't it?"

David reached over and put his arm around her. A smile touched his lips. "You always have a verse, don't you? Just like Mother did. Yes, that's what it says alright. I know the desire of our hearts. To get Starr back, that's what we want. And for you and Josh to come back safely. Let's pray for that right now."

"I think that's a good idea." The two held onto each other as they prayed. David gave her a strong hug. "You can keep on praying. Somehow I feel we're gonna get her back. It'll take the leadership of God. You know how hard it is to track anyone in this part of the world which consists of solid rock."

"God won't let us down." Miriam said as she reached up and kissed him. Then he turned and left the room. As soon as he was gone, Miriam went over and sat down on a small handmade bed, picked up the Bible and began to search it. "Oh, God," she said, "I trust in your Word. Bring them all back safely."

"I say we go right on," Punch said stubbornly. It was almost dark before they found the trail of the abductors.

David's heart leaped when they saw the sign and they had

driven their horses as hard as was safe. Now the animals were exhausted. David looked up at the sky that was almost dark. Then shook his head. "We can't go on in the dark. We might lose the trail."

"But they're right up ahead, aren't they, David?" Josh asked. He grasped his bow in his hand and added, "Let's go on. Maybe we can catch them."

"No, it's too risky. We don't know how far ahead they are."

Punch said, "You know what this country's like. There's just one trail. If we give them another day, they'll be safe. We've got to get to them tonight!"

David was still in the falling light. He stood with his head bowed silently. Josh knew that he was praying, although Punch had no sense of this. David lifted his head then pointed, "There's a small farm over there about three miles. I used to know the people. These horses won't make it. They're going to drop in another mile or two."

"Well, what are we going to do then?" Punch demanded.

"I'm going over there to get a horse. Then I'm going to cut around parallel to the trail."

Josh grasped at once what David was saying, "You're going to get ahead of 'em?"

"Yes. You two rest the horses tonight. In the morning see that they're fed good and then come along on the trail. You'll be behind them and I'll be in front of them. They can't get off that trail too far."

"We'll be separated," Punch complained. "What good will that do? These may be pretty rough fellows. I'd like to keep my head on my shoulders."

There was a short argument, but David prevailed. He turned to Josh and said, "You be careful in the morning. Punch is right. These are bad fellows. But, the Lord will be with us." He patted Josh on the shoulder and gave Punch a look. "Watch out for him. Don't rush in blindly. If you come up to them, stay well behind."

"What will you be doing?"

"I don't know, I'll have to make a plan as I go. Take care of these horses."

David left abruptly and Josh and Punch made a campfire and ate. Punch said, "Better sleep. It's gonna be a hard chase tomorrow."

Josh answered, "alright," and then lay down in his blankets. He was excited and a little afraid. He had seen death in his young life and knew that many boys, no older than he, had been killed in these border wars; but somehow he was not afraid. He was tired and his body seemed to have been beaten, the ride had been so hard, but he felt like a man and went to sleep almost instantly.

David made his way under the stars, grateful for their light. When he reached the farm he called out, "Hello in the house!" and at once a hail came to him, "Hello. Who's there?" David walked in and found an old friend named Obie, short for Obadiah. Obie, a farmer, was a small dark man, with a thin nose and light brown eyes. "I've got to have a horse, Obie."

"This time of the night?" Obie questioned. "Where're you going in the middle of the night?"

David sketched the situation and Obie's eyes grew larger. "I know Starr Omega. I met her the first time she ever came to this country. Let me get you a good horse. I'll go with you."

"No, it's too dangerous, Obie. You've got a family. Just get me a horse and I'll make out."

Thirty minutes later David moved out. He had talked at length with Obie about the trail and had discovered that there was one that paralleled the main trail. "Keep your eye out for a campfire. Maybe you'll be able to sneak up on them," Obie said. "I hope you get them, David. I sure like that Starr girl."

David smiled down at the small man. "Thanks, Obie. You might say a prayer for me."

"I'll do that. you can bet on it."

David turned the horse, a solid buckskin, who seemed eager

to move. "I hope you're a good one, Boy," David murmured, slapping him on the shoulder. "Let's go!"

The moon rose steadily and David picked his way along the secondary trail. Overhead the stars glittered down on him as they shed their tiny points of light. They were joined by the brightness of the moon. David kept his head up, constantly searching the country. *Won't do me any good to walk into an ambush*, he thought. *That wouldn't help Starr any.* The problem was he had to make time, and to make time he had to take chances. For hours he rode steadily and then decided to pull over to the main trail. *They must have gotten this far, at least*, he thought. David crossed over a small canyon, passed through a patch of scrub trees, and came upon the main trail. He turned his horse then forty-five minutes later pulled up abruptly. A tiny flicker of light was ahead of him. He took a sharp breath and held the nervous horse in hand. "That might be them," he said to himself. "No way of telling."

He moved ahead until the light grew larger and guided the horse into a small box canyon. Carefully, he hobbled the horse and looked at the small stream that ran through it. "You'll be alright here," he said to the horse. He pulled his bow from behind the saddle, along with a quiver of arrows, slipped them on and moved out into the darkness. He did not approach straightly down the main trail but moved to his left. A row of trees paralleled the trail. He flitted from trunk-to-trunk. Keeping well hidden, he always kept the fire in sight, then he paused and looked down into the canyon. Although he was still a hundred yards away from the fire, he could see figures moving. "I have to get closer," he muttered. He knew that the men he was following would be on guard. Therefore, he moved silently, "stalking" as if he were on the trail of a dangerous animal. Finally, when he was no more than a hundred feet away, he could hear the voices of the two. He recognized the voice of Abbadon.

"That's bad news," David muttered. "He knows this country." He strained his eyes and was rewarded by the sight of Starr who was sitting opposite Abbadon. The light from the campfire caught her face and he could make out her features. He drew a deep sigh of relief. "At least she's alright." He looked across from Abbadon and saw another man who was sitting back in the shadows. He could see little of the man and said to himself, "I'll never have a better chance than this." Standing there wondering how to attack he thought. *I could get one of them*, he thought, *with an arrow, but that would alert the other one. That won't do. They'll have to go to sleep eventually, though. I'll have to sneak in, finish one of them off quietly and then deal with the other.*

While it was not much of a plan, it was the best he could do. Moving from point-to-point, he made his way down until he was no farther than fifty feet away. He heard the voice of the man in the darkness say, "One of us will have to stay awake."

Abbadon said, "No one is out there."

"Maybe not—maybe so. You go to sleep. I'll take the first watch."

Abbadon grumbled, but rolled up in a blanket and grew still.

David crept closer. He still could not see the man who was sitting in the darkness. He was a little taken by surprise when Starr asked, "Why are you doing this, Mingo?"

The man called Mingo moved closer. He picked up some more firewood, tossed it into the fire and looked around. "Shouldn't have a fire. Like putting out a sign saying, anyone who wants to come in can do so." He looked over at Starr and said, "I'm doing it to get out of prison."

"Get out of prison?"

"Yes, I know this country. They said I could go free if I'd bring you in."

"Why were you in prison?"

"For being different. I didn't exactly agree with those who ran the City."

"I don't either," Starr said quickly. "I was one of them once. I was a Reliever."

"A Reliever, that's a laugh. How many did you kill?" His voice was sardonic and Starr dropped her head. She let the silence run on until Mingo said, "Never mind, it's not important."

"Yes, it is important. I didn't realize what I was doing," she said. "They told me it was right and good to relieve people when they were old and sick. It was better for them. And I believed them." She went on to explain how she had never felt comfortable with what she was doing. Then I came out here and met David and his parents. They're different out here." She hesitated then said, "And I met the Lord Jesus Christ."

At once Mingo turned to stare at her. David could see his face. It was a strong face, the eyes deep-set and the lips drawn in a tight line. "You're one of those Neo-Crossbearers. No wonder they want you back."

Starr saw the hardness of the man and knew it was hopeless to argue. So she said no more. Finally Mingo rose and said, "I'm going to take a little walk. Don't try to get away. There's no where to run to." He gave her one look, then moved away silently.

From the way he moved, David knew that he was a skilled woodsman. *I'll have to be careful with him,* David thought. He waited, trying to think of a plan. *I could sneak down and knock Abbadon in the head. That'd leave only one to deal with. But if I get caught, they'll both have me.*

Desperately he tried to resolve his plan. He had seen the man called Mingo go off toward the north. He glanced down and saw that Starr was sitting quietly and Abbadon was motionless. He was snoring and David made up his mind. *This may be the only chance I'll get.* He moved ahead, careful not to step on anything that would give him away. Soon he was less than twenty-five feet away. His greatest fear was that when Starr saw him she would cry out. *She's got to recognize me*, he thought. He pulled off his hat and stepped out into the illumination cast by the fire and saw her look toward him. Her lips opened and at once he shook his head violently and clapped his hand over his mouth as a sign.

Starr had been shocked to see David step out but at once she recognized the danger of the moment. She shot a glance at Abbadon and then looked back to David. She nodded and came up with a smile. Then she looked in the direction that Mingo had taken and pointed.

David nodded. He moved forward and, stepping quietly, stood beside the sleeping form of the bandit. *It would be easy to kill him here.* David pulled out a knife and held it for a moment, but he could not bring himself to kill a helpless, sleeping man. Instead, he replaced the knife, reached over and picked up a large heavy stick that had been gathered for firewood. It was three inches thick and green. He held it in his hand, trying it, then glanced over at Starr. Still, he hesitated. A thing like that could kill a man. He knew Abbadon to be a ruthless killer but this was not David's nature. He put the stick down, pulled the knife again. Carefully, he put the knife on Abbadon's throat. At once the big man jumped and his eyes flew open. "Lie still, Abbadon," David said. "I don't want to have to kill you."

Abbadon's eyes blinked and he felt the cold steel on his throat. "Don't—don't kill me," he whispered.

"Roll over and put your hands behind your back," David commanded.

When this was done, David reached into his pocket and came out with a small cord that he always carried as part of his equipment. He had just reached out to tie the hands of the man when Starr cried, "David—look out!"

David glanced up to see a form hurtling toward him. He had no chance. It was the second man and David saw that the man called Mingo had a sword that was flashing right toward his head. He parried the blow with a knife and at the same time managed to reach up and grab the man's tunic. With a sharp hard thrust he threw him over his head. Mingo fell heavily to the ground but was up in a moment. Abbadon, aware that he was free, rolled over and came up with a knife in his hand. David, at once, reached down and picked up the club that he had dropped. As Abbadon came in he swung the club catching the man on the side of the head. Abbadon fell, scrambling to the ground, but got to his feet. Blood was streaming down his face and he lunged out, away from David's blade. He stumbled out into the darkness but David had no time for Mingo was on him. David only had time to turn; but this time Mingo had pulled a knife from his belt. The blade flashed by the flickering light of the fire. David felt a quick pain along his arm where the blade raked, slicing through the cloth in the soft part of his underarm.

Mingo drew back the knife to send home the death blow but in doing so he had turned his back on Starr Omega. He did not see her leap to her feet, then picked up a heavy stone and raise it over her head. Without hesitation, she brought it down on top of his unprotected skull and he dropped unconscious at once.

"David!" Starr ran to David who held her with one hand. He was searching the darkness for Abbadon. He heard the sound of a horse being ridden away at top speed then he said, "He got away! But I couldn't kill him in cold blood." He looked down at the still form and said, "Let's see about this one."

Starr was horrified to see that the back of the man's head was wet with blood. "Is he—is he dead?"

"No, but his skull's pretty well messed up. I think he'll be alright."

"We can't leave him here," Starr whispered.

"No, let me see if Abbadon left any of the other horses."

He moved into the darkness and was relieved to find that there were two horses. He led them back into the firelight and said, "We'll have to get away from here. I don't know if he could get help, but he might. Come on!"

"What about him?"

"I'll put him on this horse and lead it. You get on that one."

Starr mounted the horse and watched as David carefully tied the unconscious figure of Mingo to the other. He turned to her and said, "Come on. Punch and Josh are back there, but we've got to move on." He walked out into the darkness and Starr watched as the head of the unconscious man lolled with the movement of the horse. She had never struck anyone before in anger. Now she was terrified lest he die. She found herself praying for him and was surprised. She thought, *I could never have prayed for a man like that before I became a Christian.*

Chapter Twelve

The Captives

"What do you mean, Mingo was taken and possibly killed?"

Leo Zeta's face was the color of a ripe tomato. He was a man who carried a great deal of anger inside him and had not troubled himself to conceal or refrain from explosive outbursts of anger. Now, the wrath that had been building up in him exploded like a volcano. He stared at Abbadon, his pale eyes glowing like live coals. "The fool got himself killed trying to take one small woman?"

Abbadon shifted uneasily. He felt out of place in the grandiose office and the City as a whole. His whole life had been spent in the Fields and he wished that he were back there. He had gone to give his report to a Border Guard; but had not been permitted to return to his village. Instead the guard had taken him to the Domed City and now he stood trying to meet the eyes of Leo Zeta.

"I—it wasn't my fault," he blurted out. "We never—I woke up with a blade at my throat. If I had done anything I would have been killed."

"It may not be too late for that!" Zeta gritted his teeth and stared at the hulking man. "Now, tell me all of it. Did you get the woman?"

"Yes, we had her. One more day and we would have been out of the Badlands but—they caught us at night."

"Who is 'they'? Were you overtaken by a band?"

Abbadon was tempted to lie, but realized that this was no man to lie to. Leo Zeta's reputation had come even as far as the Fields. Abbadon blurted out, "Well, not exactly. He caught us off guard."

"Oh, one man caught you off guard?" Zeta said sarcastically.

"I know it sounds bad, but when I woke up and that knife was at my throat, there was nothing I could do. He would have killed me like a chicken!"

"Well, go on. What's the rest of it?"

"I didn't see the rest of it. Mingo came roaring in and I slipped out from under the knife. But then, when Mingo went down I had to get away."

"They took Mingo that easy? Who did it?"

"Well, the woman, I think. I don't know, really. There was just the two of them, David and Omega. But, I was all alone out there so I got on a horse and got away. At least you know where they are," he said quickly trying to appease the angry official. "I can take you right back there."

Zeta shook his head in disgust. "And you think they're just going to wait until we get there? You're going back alright and you're going to find them. If you don't, I'll show you what happens to people who don't cooperate." He punched the button on his desk and when a guard stepped in he said, "Take him away and hold him. We'll be needing him." He ignored Abbadon's protest and, when the door slammed, he sat down and thought hard. More and more it was becoming apparent that taking the woman was not going to be easy. The Gunships had failed and now Mingo. What was left? He rose to his feet, realizing that he would have to go and tell Saul Lambda about the failure of the mission. *He doesn't have to know it all,* Zeta thought. *I'll put the blame on Mingo and Abbadon. It was his way of avoiding responsibility. His fertile mind framed his report as he walked down the hall.*

There was nothing at first but a large pool of darkness. He seemed to be down under fathoms of ink-black water. Somehow far above his head there was light, air, and even laughter. He could sense all this, but when he tried to break through, the water pressed down, like earth on his chest.

I'm buried alive! He thought wildly. He tried to move his arms and hands to uncover what felt like a mound of dirt, but it was no use. Sometimes he'd hear the laughter, then the sound of voices. He would try to break free from the icy cold unconsciousness that he floated in. Sometimes he would sense warm hands on his face or body and he would want to cry out for help. Then his mind would frame the words, "Help me! I can't get out! I'm buried alive!" but he was unable to speak.

It seemed like he had been buried in this ocean of oblivion for days or months. Years, even centuries may have rolled over him. The pyramids could have been built, or it could have been a mere matter of minutes. Time had ceased to exist and Mingo was grasped by fear that somehow this was permanent. That forever, he would be in this grave. He had heard of hell, a place that the Neo-Crossbearers believe in. The startling thought came to him, *this is hell and I am not out of it.* He had never believed in such things. He believed that when a man died, he was as an animal. Now, however, he knew that he was alive. He knew that there was a world. He knew that people were laughing and talking, eating and drinking, while he was cut off from it.

One pair of hands and one voice seemed softer than the rest. The hands would come, from time-to-time and he would feel their coolness on his forehead and face. The voice, too, was soft. He could not understand the words, but when the voice came, he was relieved. He had the feeling that in those hands and in that voice there was a kind of salvation, and a prayer that rose from him—Mingo—who had never said a prayer in his whole life.

Then, there came a different kind of sensation. He did not understand much about it, but as the soft voice spoke, he suddenly seemed to rise out of the depths of unconsciousness. He became aware of his body. He could feel cool sheets under him. He could feel the pressure of a pillow pressing against the back of his head. He was also aware of a ripping pain that tore through his head when he tried to move.

He could smell things, too. The odors of the feathers in the pillow came to him. He could smell the scent of earth, fallow and dark and dank. And over all this, he could smell something pleasant, like a flower.

I'm alive, he thought, *I can feel things, I can smell.* He opened his eyes to a slit and was aware that someone was bending over him. The features were blurred, and at first he could see only a pale outline. There was a light, and it seemed to flicker with an amber glow. He shut his eyes tightly, and when he opened them again he saw that it was a woman's face. She was bathing him—he felt the cool water as she mopped his neck and shoulders. He saw that she had very black hair that hung down her back, and her eyes were dark.

"Where is this place?" he managed to whisper. His lips were dry and his voice was raspy from the lack of use.

Miriam, who had been bathing the wounded man, blinked with surprise and almost dropped the cloth. Her eyes flew open and she said with a startled voice, "You're awake!"

Again Mingo whispered, "Where is this?"

"Don't try to move," Miriam instructed. "You've been badly hurt."

In echo to her words, the pain ran through his head. He gasped, but held very still. "What's wrong with me?" He coughed, which caused his head to move and the pain to return. "What's wrong with my head?"

"You had an accident, but you're going to be alright."

"How long have I been here?" Mingo asked. He seemed to be growing stronger now and could see more clearly that the young woman was wearing a simple garment made out of cotton, a form of tunic, with a leather belt around her waist. She was young, no more than eighteen or nineteen, he judged, and very attractive. He was suddenly aware that he was more hungry and thirsty than he'd ever been in his life. "Can I have a drink?" he asked.

"Oh yes," said Miriam. "Here! Do you think you can sit up?"

"Yes." Mingo struggled to a sitting position, ignoring the pain that seemed to wrack his skull. As the girl moved across the room to pour water from an earthen jug, he looked around and saw that he was in a cave of some sort. There was furniture in it—not much, just the bed he was lying on, and a rough table and a chair. Items of clothing hung from pegs on the wall. To his left he saw that the cave apparently had a turn where he could see sunlight shining across the opening. He had no time to see more when Miriam held a cup to his lips which he grasped and guzzled down thirstily.

"Not so fast! Take it in small sips," she said. "You can have all you want." Miriam refilled the cup twice and then asked, "How do you feel?"

"I feel like a mountain fell on my head." Suddenly, memory came back and Mingo grew tense. He realized that he had been overcome by the attackers at the camp. He wondered briefly about Abbadon, then asked, "Am I a prisoner?"

"You're a patient. My name is Miriam."

"But I can't leave here, can I? I wouldn't get far."

Miriam hesitated. "I suppose you're a prisoner. There's a guard outside, but you couldn't go anywhere anyway. You're not able to walk." She said, "Are you hungry? Can you eat something?"

At the question he suddenly realized that he was hungry. "Yes, anything," he said.

"I'll get something. I don't think you'd better get out of bed though. Not for a while."

"Alright."

Miriam left the cave and said to the man who was standing guard, "He's awake. I'm going to get him something hot to eat."

"Alright, I'll watch him."

She went to the main cave and found Starr inside. "He's awake," she said, "And he's hungry."

"Take him some of this stew," said Starr. "Or, I'll go with you. I want to talk to him anyway." The two women put together a simple meal of stew and bread and also fruit. They walked to the smaller cave. As she entered, Starr was surprised at the bright eyes of the man. "Well, you *are* doing better, Mingo."

"How do you know my name?"

"That's what the other man called you."

"Is he dead?"

"Oh, no. He got away on one of the horses."

Hope leaped into Mingo when he realized that Abbadon might bring back help. He said nothing, but when the food was put before him, he began to eat. Finally, he grew tired and asked, "How long have I been here?"

"Almost a week. We thought you were going to die. You got fever and you couldn't come out of your unconsciousness. You were in a coma." Miriam said.

Starr was observing him. He was cool enough, it seemed. There was a steadiness in his gaze. He focused his blue eyes on her and studied her carefully. "I'm sorry you got hurt," she said.

Mingo was surprised at the statement. "You shouldn't be. If I hadn't been stopped, you'd be in the hands of the authorities by now. You know what that means."

"Yes, I know what that means," Starr nodded. "But still, I am glad you're alright."

There was a silence for a moment and then Starr continued, "We've changed locations. I don't think help will be coming for you, Mingo."

As if he were speaking to someone else he said, "What are you going to do with me? I'm kind of excess baggage. You can't afford to keep me here, and you can't afford to let me go."

It was a problem that David and Starr had talked about and decided, "We'll have to keep him. He found us once, he could do it again. We'll have to keep on the move, too. Abbadon's likely to bring back help."

Starr looked at the young man and said, "You'll be well treated. Somehow it'll all work out. Let me know if you need anything."

She turned and left the room and Miriam asked quickly, "Would you like anything else to eat?"

"No." He was growing sleepy again and fear came upon him. As he dropped off he was filled with apprehension that he might drop back into that deep, dark ocean and forget everything. Nevertheless his sleep was easy and quiet. It came to him almost at once, like a baby.

Miriam looked down at the still face and thought for a long time. She had taken care of Mingo since he had been brought in—she and Starr Omega. And now he seemed to be more helpless than before. She had been afraid that he would die, but now that he would live, she wondered what will happen to him.

"I'd like to get out of here a little. Do you think they might let me do that?"

It was three days after Mingo had first awakened. His strength had returned rapidly and the pain in his head had grown less severe. Only when he moved quickly did it come now. He had been well treated but, as with the prison in the Tower, he had grown restless.

He had asked Miriam the question as she had come to bring him his food. Miriam stared at him and replied, I don't know,

Mingo. I'll have to ask David and some of the Elders. If you give you're word, they might let you out of the cave."

"My word?"

"Yes, your word that you won't try to run away."

Mingo smiled. "I don't think they'd be likely to take *my* word. I'm the one who came to steal Starr from them." He glanced at her curiously. He was standing up now and saw that she was almost as tall as he. She was slender and well-shaped. And he knew that she had a quick and active mind. She also had a sense of humor. "I didn't know people believed in things like that anymore."

"Oh, yes. At least out here in the Fields they do. When it's said of someone, 'He has a word,' that means you can depend on him to do what he says."

Mingo thought that over carefully. "Well, I don't know if I have a word or not, but I'd like to get out of this place."

"I'll go ask David. You eat. It'll do you good."

Miriam left and Mingo sat down on the rough bed and ate the food. It was a vegetable with cold beef. He ate it hungrily. His strength was almost fully-returned now, and he could walk without the dizziness. Finally, he finished and stood to his feet stretching. He was like a caged animal and, despite the pain in his head, he would walk the floor for hours. He thought of the hours that Miriam had sat beside him. Sometimes they would talk—he had learned that she was a simple girl who had grown up in a village in the Fields. He had also discovered that she had lost her parents to their enemies in the City. He had learned all about David and Josh and also Miriam.

"She seems interested in me," he muttered as he waited impatiently. "I've told her more about myself than I've ever told anyone in my life, not that there's that much to tell." His mind turned to the idea of escape but he quickly dismissed the thought.

"Shouldn't be too hard," he said, "Except that David. He's a pretty hard nut. I don't know what to make of him."

He was still thinking when Miriam came back with a smile on her face. "David says you can go about the village, but not outside, and he wants your word that you won't run away. Just give it to me. He said that would be alright."

"Well, I promise you I won't run away until we've had our walk. Tomorrow we may have to renegotiate."

Miriam laughed, "That's alright. Come on. The two of them walked outside and she said, "It's cold today. I think winter's coming."

"Feels good to me," he said. "I always like this time of the year."

The two of them walked around the village as Mingo was well aware that he was being watched. Not by Miriam, particularly, but the man called "Punch" was trailing along behind them. He finally turned and asked, "Are you following me?"

Punch stood with the slingshot in his hand, and said, "Who? Me? I'm just taking a walk."

"I'll bet. How far would I get if I tried to make a break?"

Punch shrugged, "I don't think you'll do that."

"No, I don't think I will. Not today, anyway."

The walk was the best thing that had happened to him since he had gone down in the fight. He gingerly touched the bandage on his head and sighed, "I guess I'm going to live. I never thought I'd be brought down by a woman. Teach me not to turn my back on one again." He smiled down at her and chided, "Would you hit a man on the head with a rock, Miriam?"

"I might," she said. "We don't know what we'll do until we're faced with trouble."

"You're right about that," he said soberly. It brought back his history and he grew quiet. He became so quiet, that finally Miriam noticed it.

"What's wrong? I thought you'd be glad to get outside."

"It's just another prison," he shrugged. "I like this one better though."

"What was it like in that jail?"

"Rather not talk about it," he said. "The whole City's a jail to me. I grew up out here." He'd told her this before and now she drew stories out of him as they walked. Punch was always lurking in the background, with slingshot in hand. So Mingo knew there was no hope of escape. "Besides," he said humorously, "I've given my word. Haven't done that in a long time."

For an hour they roamed around the village of tents. The village had only the two caves, but the tents sheltered the others.

"Tell me about these people," he questioned idly.

Miriam began identifying the villagers. Finally, she pointed to a short, young man who was walking with a young woman. "That's Isaac and Mary," she said. "I expect they'll get married."

"Who's the big hulking fellow over there that looks mad about the whole thing," Mingo inquired, gesturing toward a tall, muscular man who was watching the couple.

"Oh, that's Cain. He's in love with Mary."

"Why doesn't he take her? He's bigger than Isaac."

Miriam looked at him with astonishment. "Why, because she's in love with Isaac!"

"He doesn't look like a very good bet to me. This is a hard country and he's so short. Cain over there now, he's big enough to take care of himself."

"We don't do it that way out here. When a man and women are in love, they take each other as they are."

"I've heard about this love business. I saw some of it from time to time, but I never could understand it. Tell me about it."

"You're teasing me!"

"I guess so. I'm one of the roughs. No woman could put up with me for ten minutes."

Miriam smiled and a dimple appeared in her cheek. "I've heard men say that before. My brother used to say it, but now Starr can get him to do anything."

"Is that right? He's a pretty tough fellow. I'm surprised he'd let a woman push him around and give him orders."

"Oh, Starr doesn't give him orders. She makes him think that *he* thought of whatever it is."

"That's the secret, is it?"

"That's one of them." Miriam suddenly looked at him and asked, "Haven't you ever had a sweetheart?"

The question made Mingo nervous and he shrugged, "I've known a few women, but none that could ever make me do anything I didn't want to do."

"It doesn't work that way, I don't think," Miriam said more seriously. "When two people love each other they're interested in seeing the best for the other. Starr wants what's best for David. David wants what's best for Starr. They give up themselves to have each other."

It was a new concept and Mingo thought about it. For several days, he kept giving his word on a daily basis. Soon he knew all the members of the Remnant and was surprised at how they seemed to accept him even though they knew he was an enemy.

At first he had some difficulty with Josh. The boy had stared at him with animosity until Mingo said, "You don't like me, Josh."

"No, that's right, I don't."

"That's good. A man should say what he thinks. I'm glad to see you learned that lesson."

Nevertheless, Josh was fascinated by Mingo. For one thing, Mingo had been all over the Fields and even beyond. For years he had been a member of a band of hunters. He knew all about that kind of life. Later, after Josh grew closer to him, he asked, "Why did you come to get Starr?"

"Because they offered me life," he said. "I was in a prison and I wasn't going to live long. I believe I would of died of my own will, if it's possible for a man to do that."

Mingo was sitting beside the creek watching Josh pull in small fish. He waved his hands at the blue sky and said, "I needed to be out like this and they put me in a cage. I don't think you should do that even to an animal."

"I don't either," Josh said. He pulled another fish in, took it off the hook and put it in the canvas bag. "These aren't very big fish," he said.

"No. They're good to eat, and you're a good fisherman, Josh. Sometime I'd like to take you up in the high country. There are fish up there that you wouldn't believe. And they put up quite a fight."

Josh's eyes lit up. "Really? I'd like to go there. Maybe you could . . ."

Mingo grinned at the boy's break in speech. "I'm not likely to take you there as long as I'm a prisoner, but things change."

"Do you think you might ever go back to the City?"

A cloud crossed Mingo's face. "Never! I'd die before I'd go back there!"

Josh was fascinated and later talked to Miriam about the prisoner. "He knows all about hunting and fishing and even tracked the big mountain lions over in the north. Got them with a bow, like I use. He said he might take me there sometime, if things ever change."

"He must be quite a good hunter."

Josh stared at her. "You two talk all the time. What do you talk about, Miriam?"

"Oh, just things." Miriam flushed slightly and said, "Don't get too fond of Mingo."

"Why not?"

"He'll be going away some day and you'd be lonesome and miss him."

"But you talk all the time and you like him. Don't you, Miriam?"

Miriam's flush grew richer and she said firmly, "Maybe so, but it can't come to anything."

Later, after Josh had left, she suddenly realized the question had come sharply to her. She rebuked herself saying, "I better take a dose of my own medicine. It wouldn't be smart to get too fond of Mingo. After all, he's an enemy—even if he doesn't seem like one.

Chapter Thirteen

"I Thee Wed . . . "

"Have you noticed how Josh has taken to Mingo?" David asked as he and Starr walked along the bank of a small creek that bubbled over smooth stones. The two had found time for a walk just before twilight when the faint twinkle of stars was discernible.

"Yes," Starr replied. She hesitated, then shook her head. "I'm not sure if it's a good thing. I mean, after all, Mingo isn't one of us."

"No, that's true," David admitted. They slowly walked along, both preoccupied. Sitting down on a fallen log, they watched the blood-red sun sink behind the mountains. There was a quietness over the land. Somewhere far off a dog barked, but when he stopped, it seemed as though nothing had stirred.

Finally, David turned to Starr and said, "I'm not sure what to do about it. Matter of fact, I'm not sure what to do about Mingo."

"Have you tried to talk to him?"

"Yes, and to tell the truth, I like the fellow. He's a lot like me in some ways."

Starr's eyes twinkled for a moment. "Oh, he's much better looking than you," she chided.

"You think so, do you?" David playfully reached over and caught her hair, turning her face towards his. "I'll make you pay for that! It may be the truth, but I don't like to hear my girl saying it."

"Ow, you're pulling my hair." Starr reached up and put her hand behind David's neck. "Please, I was only teasing."

He released her hair and she shoved him over the log. Laughing, she ran along the path. He scrambled to his feet, caught up with her, then turned her face towards him. "It's going to take a lot of patience living with you, Woman," he said. Then he held her tight for a moment, kissed her on the cheek, and smoothed her hair, "But I think I can put up with you for the next forty or fifty years."

It was a good time for Starr Omega. She had been brought up in a rigid system, devoid of love, with a system of values based on egotism. All her life in the City she had been taught in one form or another that life was successful only so long as you grasp as much as possible for your own needs and selfish desires. Looking back, she wondered with a strange sense of awe, how she had managed to escape such a terrible background. Now, as she and David held each other, there was a peace that was in her heart that had never been there when she was a child or during the days of her growing up. She had been approached by many men to become a Loving Companion, which simply meant free sexual encounters without obligation or responsibility.

Now, as they turned and walked back toward the camp, she said suddenly, "I don't know if I could be a good wife, David. I haven't had the training for it." She hesitated, "I wish I was like Miriam. She had your parents' life to look at. I don't have anything like that."

David looked down at her and smiled. "You've got a loving heart and that's what counts. You know what I think marriage really is?"

"What do you think?"

"I think a good marriage is when both parties are more interested in the other's well being than in their own. For instance, after we're married, if I want steak for supper and you want fish, you'll insist on steak and I'll insist on fish."

Starr giggled, "I hope that turns out to be our worst problem, whether to have steak or fish!" Then she sobered and nodded, "I think you're right, though. I've been in the Fields long enough and seen enough good marriages to know that that is what it is—longing for the other's comfort and well-being. I'm going to like being married," she said.

"Well, you've got two more days as a single woman. If you're gonna have a fling, you'd better have it now."

"Who would I have a fling with? Punch?"

David laughed aloud. "He'd run like a deer if you said a thing like that to him. He's not afraid of anything on this earth that I can figure out—except women."

"My old psychiatry teacher would have said his mother dropped him on his head or something. It's quite the thing in the City to blame everything that happens on our parents, or whoever raised us. No one has any guilt. It's all someone else's fault."

They reached the village and, as they did, they found that Mingo and Josh had gone out hunting.

"I think it's good that you've taken Mingo at his word—about not running away. Shows we trust him."

"Well, I hope he doesn't run away. That'd be all we need," David said. "But, I don't think he will. This is his kind of place."

Mingo and Josh had traveled over ten miles looking for a likely place to hunt the wild hogs that inhabited the forest close by. They both carried bows slung over their backs. But their main weapons were the eight-foot spears with the steel-tip heads. Josh was a little apprehensive—he had seen what wild hogs can do. But he was glad to be with Mingo, and as the two moved through the forest, he tried to imitate Mingo as much as he could. Josh had always imitated David, and still thought his brother was the best man in the whole world. But David was busy and Mingo, as a prisoner, had nothing but time on his hands. Consequently, the two gravitated toward one another.

The evergreens overhead had dropped their needles over the past hundred years forming a carpet on the ground. Thus, the feet of the two men made no sound as they wound around some of the larger trunks, Mingo always looking, his eyes never still. From time-to-time they would stop. Josh finally asked, "What are we stopping for?"

Mingo looked at the boy and grinned, "Maybe I'm tired," he said.

"No, you never get tired."

"Sure I do. I just don't let anyone know about it. But now we're stopping to listen. No way to track the pigs over these needles, but you can hear them from a long way off, just listen."

As the two stood there. Josh lifted his head and tried to shut out everything except sound. He shut his eyes and, as Mingo had told him so often, when one sense is gone you use another—it gets sharper. Now Josh could hear the wind whispering in the top of the evergreens, and far off, he could hear the faint cry of a bird making a sound almost like a scream. He listened more closely and thought he could hear the sound of running water. It was very faint, but he mentioned it to his companion. "Is that a creek I hear, Mingo?"

"You got good ears. We'll move over that way. Wherever there's water, there's bound to be game, especially in a country like this."

As they moved along, Josh was happy. He said as much to Mingo. "We've had so much fun on these hunting trips. David's too busy. But you've got lots of time."

"Sure," Mingo answered. "When you're in jail, there's not a whole lot to do."

"Aw, you're not in jail, Mingo. David lets you go anywhere you want."

"No, he doesn't. He makes me promise I won't go *anywhere*."

"Where do you want to go then?" When Mingo did not answer, Josh asked quickly, "Why don't you just stay with us? Do you have a home or family somewhere?"

After a seemingly long pause Mingo replied, "No, no family," When Mingo took so long to answer Josh felt rebuked. He moved along behind Mingo, watching the man pick each spot for his feet. Finally, Mingo said, "I like it fine here but I'm not like you people."

"What do you mean, not like us?"

"All of you are Christians. I'd fit in like a square peg in a round hole."

Josh blinked, "Well, why don't you just become a Christian then?"

Mingo gave Josh an amusing glance and then lifted his hand, "The creek must be right there."

They moved together and found a small creek no more than three or four feet across that trickled down the mountain slope. "Let's move along until we see some tracks," Mingo suggested. They moved upstream and had not gone more than a hundred yards when Mingo pointed downward. "Look, a watering hole!" The banks were worn smooth on both sides. "We'll get something here if we wait long enough." Said Mingo. "I think the pigs come here. See those prints."

The ground was hard but when Josh leaned over he saw the split hoof prints of a pig and gasped, "Boy, they're big, aren't they!"

"Yes, they are, and mean, too."

"Maybe we can get 'em with the arrows."

"That's our best shot. Those fellows are pretty rough when you try to handle them with anything else." He looked around and said, "We'll get in those bushes right over there. Sooner or later, something will come along. I'd rather it'd be a deer, though."

The two concealed themselves in the bushes and sat down to wait. "The hardest part of hunting," Mingo said, "Is doing nothing, just waiting." Silence fell on the place and, when nothing showed for half an hour, Mingo said, as if there had been no intervening time, "I don't think I could do it."

Josh blinked in surprise. "Do what?" he demanded.

"Become a Christian, like you are; like David and Starr and almost everyone else in this group."

"Why not?"

"Because I've listened to enough of the preaching that goes on in the services to find out that when a man becomes a Christian he gives up being his own man." He paused and his strong bronzed face looked thoughtful. He gazed over at the boy who was standing holding his bow. Mingo thought also about when he had been that age, how wild he'd been, how eager to taste life. *Some of that's been taken out of me*, he thought. *I hope Josh doesn't have the hard time I've had.*

Josh had been thinking about what the Mingo had said. "What do you mean," he said, fingering the bow almost nervously. "David hasn't given up being a man."

"In a way he has. He's promised to be obedient to Jesus Christ. All Christians do. Isn't that what it's all about?"

Josh himself had found the Lord when he was twelve-years old. It had been a simple matter of calling upon God, asking Him for forgiveness. And he could still remember to this day the peace that rushed into his soul when he had done that. Now he looked at Mingo and said, "Why, it's not like that at all."

"You do have to promise to obey God, don't you? To do what He commands?"

"Well, sure," Josh blurted out, "But that's not hard."

"It would be for me. I've always done exactly what I wanted to do."

Josh was a wise young man for his years. He had been studying Mingo for some time now and asked the one question that was exactly right. "Are you happy then, Mingo, doing exactly what you want to do?"

Mingo shot an astonished glance at the young man. He had not realized that Josh had been so astute. Uttering a half laugh, he shook his head, "No I'm not. But I don't know if I'd be any happier doing what God wanted me to do."

Josh wanted to help the man. He longed to see him find happiness. He knew instinctively that Mingo had had a hard life. Now he said slowly, "I don't know much about these things Mingo—but I know one thing . . ." He hesitated, then ran his hand along the polished wood of the bow. He had forgotten that they were on a hunt for the matter at hand was far more important. "I know that everywhere I look, when people are together, you have to give up part of yourself."

"Give up part of yourself?" Mingo looked puzzled. "What does that mean?"

"If I have a friend, I have to think about him," Josh insisted. "I can't always do just what I want to do. Sometimes I have to do what he wants to do. And the same thing is true when people get married. If a man is alone, he can go hunting when he wants to, or do anything else. But if he has a wife, he has to think about her. Then when children come along, he has to think about them."

"Sounds like a good reason for not getting tied down."

"I don't think so. I wouldn't want to be someone without a friend. When I get old like you, I wouldn't want to be all alone. I need people."

The simple statement touched a cord in Mingo and he stared over at the boy silently. *I need people.* The words echoed in his mind and he turned his face away from Josh so that the boy could not see how it affected him. All of his life he had been alone. He had known other people. He had had a man or two that he was close to. He had known women, but only in the most casual sort of way.

He'd had no memory of a family life. He had been raised by strangers, thrown out on his own when he was only a boy. It had been a hard life. He finally turned to Josh and said, "I've never known anything like that so it's hard for me to judge."

Josh started to answer and then suddenly he broke off, "Listen! Something's coming!"

Both man and boy notched their arrows and stood alertly waiting. "Pigs, I think. They don't sound like anything else."

In five minutes six pigs emerged from the brush across the creek. They sniffed the air and uttered their peculiar grunting noises. One of them slashed with his yellowish fangs at another, bringing out a squeal. Three of them were large, ugly animals. The other three were females or younger boars. Josh could not tell which. He was watching the leader carefully, a monster of a beast. He had small, reddish eyes and huge curving tusks that could kill a man in one slash. They were quick, too, Josh could tell. He had never been on a boar hunt before, though he loved the taste of the meat.

Mingo kept his eye on the small herd and picked out the largest of the animals. He whispered to Josh, "Take the one on the right of the big boy. Ready?"

Josh whispered, "Yes," and raised his bow, then drew it back to the full length. When Mingo said 'now' he released the arrow. It went straight and true, driving into the body of the animal he had aimed at. Instantly, the pigs began squealing angrily. The animal Josh had hit fell on his side, kicking wildly. "We've got 'em," Josh yelled, and without thinking threw down his bow and ran out of the cover of the trees.

"Josh! Come back!" Mingo yelled.

Josh stopped instantly; realizing that the third boar was still very much alive. The animal saw him at once and with a terrible scream, his feet clattering on the hard ground, headed straight for him. As he approached he looked as big as a house. Josh knew that there was no time to turn. He knew those razor sharp tusks would kill him. He tried to turn but his foot slipped and he fell. With horror he saw that the boar was almost on him.

Then, as Josh lay there, something moved. He had time only to see that it was Mingo carrying one of the spears. The boar that was charging at them weighed more than Mingo did, close to two-hundred pounds of squealing fury. Josh watched as Mingo leaped over, kneeled down and put the butt of the spear in the ground. He had told Josh once before, "You can't hold 'em off with your hands. Get your spear in the ground and let him run himself into it."

The boar hit the steel tipped edge of the spear. It entered his chest but he seemed to feel no pain. He squealed horribly, then twisted his body so that the spear was wrenched from Mingo's hand. With the spear still protruding, the boar threw himself awkwardly at the pair. He slashed with his tusks, catching Mingo's boot and ripping it from sole to top. He also caught part of the flesh—but it was his last effort. He swayed and seemed to be seeking breath. His eyes seemed dulled over and then he slumped down, his legs collapsing. He trembled for a moment, the blood pouring out of the wound until the grunts died away to silence.

Josh got up, his legs trembling and weak. "I thought . . . he had me . . . that time! He would have if you hadn't got him, Mingo."

Mingo took a deep breath and got to his feet. He looked down at his foot and saw where the tusks had ripped his boot. "He got me a little in the leg. Not bad." Mingo's voice was not steady. He looked down at the dying animal and swallowed, "We were lucky. He could have killed both of us, Josh."

Josh was almost speechless. Now that it was over, he realized his mistake. "I don't know how to thank you," he said. "I was a fool to step out like that."

Mingo saw that the boy was pale and his lips were trembling. "Let's sit down. My legs are pretty shaky."

The two sat down, Josh not wanting to admit how sick he felt. His brush with death had happened so quickly that he had not had time to think about it. He sat quietly and found that he was breathing very rapidly. "Take slow, deep breaths," Mingo said. He slapped Josh on the shoulder saying, "These things are always worse after they're over. You don't have time to think while it's happening."

Josh took a deep breath and forced himself to say, "If it had been a little different, we might be dead. Makes a fellow think, doesn't it?"

Mingo looked down at the rip on his boot and the tiny line of blood where the tusk had grazed him. He knew what would have happened if the boar had caught him squarely. He thought of death with a jolt, then nodded slowly, "Yes, it does."

◆　　　　◆　　　　◆

The entire Remnant was gathered together for the wedding of Starr. The ceremony took place in an open spot and the words were spoken by Obadiah. No one had bothered to dress up. Even Starr wore a simple short tunic, and her hair was braided with wild flowers that Miriam had found.

Obadiah began by speaking of what it meant to be married. He spoke of how when a man and woman come together, they come together forever.

"Even among animals, which have no souls, we find some that mate for life. Those that do not are merely beast-like. It is sad when men and women become no more than beasts. But you, David and Starr," He paused and looked at the couple who stood before him. "I require that you will love each other as long as you live. When one gets sick, the other must tend him. When the hard times come, you must cling together. This will not be for a day, or a month or even a year, but as long as you live . . ."

No one listened to the words of the preacher any more than Mingo. He had spent much of his life out in the Fields and was aware of marriage customs. It had always seemed strange to him. He had been brought up among people with rough manners. To Mingo the outcasts in the Fields were not much more than animals. And, as Obadiah spoke of loving forever, it struck a chord in Mingo. As he listened to Obadiah his eyes were on David and Starr, wondering what they were thinking.

Starr treasured the words. She held David's hand as Obadiah said to repeat, "David, I thee wed, and promise to love thee all the days of my life."

She listened as David repeated the same words. They held hands while Obadiah laid out their duties, stressing faithfulness, loyalty and most of all love.

Then Obadiah announced, "You are now husband and wife. May God pour His blessings upon you and may you bring forth many children."

David kissed his bride, his lips firmly placed on hers. Once again Starr felt the peace and security that David had brought into her life.

And then there was a loud applause as everyone came laughing to shake their hands and kiss the bride. Starr looked up and saw Punch standing to one side. Mischievously, she moved away from those who waited and to Punches complete surprise, asked, "Aren't you going to kiss the bride, Punch?"

Punch was shocked when Starr reached up, pulled his head down and kissed him. His face became as red as the evening sun. With a gasp, he turned away and stalked off toward the food. "I came to eat, not to get kissed!" he said loudly.

Starr laughed and went back to David. "He needs a wife. She'd teach him better manners."

"Is that a warning that I'm about to be instructed?" David laughed.

"You two can argue later," Miriam said. "Now it's time to eat."

It was a beautiful time for Starr. An aura of peace clung to her. Happiness shone in her eyes.

When she had time to speak with Josh, he said, "I've never seen you look so happy."

Miriam stood by and smiled, "It's supposed to be that way, Josh. Don't you remember some of the old books that said they got married and lived happily ever after?"

Starr smiled at the boy and said, "I'm glad to be a member of your family, Josh. I've never had a brother. Now I have such a handsome one."

Josh flushed and shook his head. He looked over at Mingo and said, "You wouldn't have a brother if he hadn't saved me from that wild hog."

David had come up in time to hear this and clapped Josh on the shoulder. "I'm in his debt for that. I couldn't do without you, little brother." He looked at Miriam and said, "Go over and explain to Mingo he's not supposed to stand around looking like a stone statue at a wedding. He's supposed to be celebrating."

Miriam smiled and went at once through the crowd. She found Mingo leaning back against a tree. "Come on," she said. "It's time to be foolish."

Mingo let her take his hand. He had been somewhat stunned by the simplicity of the wedding and by the obvious love he saw in the bride and the groom. "They're happy, aren't they?" he said, as Miriam led him away.

"Of course they are! Why shouldn't they be? They have each other. Isn't that the way it's supposed to be?"

Mingo was very conscious of the warmth of her hand in his. "I don't know," he said. "I've never been around a thing like this."

When they had gotten some food and had sat down Mingo asked, "When will you get married, Miriam?"

"Oh, I don't know?" She replied. The question seemed to trouble her.

Mingo looked at her curiously, "Josh tells me you've had lots of young men trying to marry you. Why didn't you take any of them?"

"I've told you before, I didn't love any of them."

"Do you think you will one day? Get married, I mean."

"Of course. God will send me someone."

The words arrested Mingo and he sat there silently, picking at the food. Finally, he turned to her and said quietly, "Well, when He does send someone, he'll be a lucky man."

His words shocked Miriam. She looked up quickly and said, "Why, Mingo! What a nice thing to say."

Mingo was not a man who had an easy time with words but he said now, as simply as he could, "I've never known anyone kinder than you, Miriam. If everyone were like you, this would be a good world." When she didn't answer he said, "And you're pretty, too, the prettiest girl I've ever seen."

Miriam was astounded, "Why, Mingo, you sound like a man courting!"

Mingo blinked with astonishment, then smiled, "I do, don't I? Well, who knows, one day it might come to that."

Miriam sat silently for a while. For some time she had been attracted to this man. Now alone with him she said to herself, *He could be a wonderful man if he'd just give his heart to God.*

Chapter Fourteen

A Command From Goel

For two weeks after the marriage of David and Starr, Mingo was in a strange mood. He could have walked away anytime and left the Remnant. But he had given his word and, although this had never been important to him before, he felt an obligation to keep it. Several times he had decided to leave, to get away, but always when the moment came, he found he couldn't do it. There was something about the group, particularly David's family, that intrigued him.

He was taken off guard therefore when, after he had shared a meal with the family, David had looked up and said with a smile, "I am releasing you from your promise, Mingo."

For one moment Mingo could not think what he meant and then it came to him. "You mean, I'm free to go?"

"That's right."

Somehow, instead of feeling relief and gladness at being relieved from his promise, Mingo felt a sense of doubt and even sadness.

"You don't look very happy, Mingo," Miriam said. "We thought it would be a good gift for you. We all talked it over."

Mingo looked at her and memories came to him of the good times they had had together. He knew by this time that whatever a man could feel for a woman, other than in just a sexual sense, he felt for Miriam. He found himself thinking about her at odd times. Thoughts of things she had said would come back to him bringing a smile to his lips. Now, however, he was in a quandary.

"Well, I thank you," he said. "It's been different living with you."

Josh looked unhappy. "Will you be leaving, Mingo?"

The question seemed to trouble Mingo. He looked down at the table not answering. "I suppose so."

"You don't have to," David said. "There's always a place for you with us."

Mingo looked up quickly. He had learned to admire and respect David more than he had any man. But now, in a troubled voice he answered, "That's good of you, David, but I'm not like you. Not like any of you." He looked around the table.

"We're not all supposed to be alike," Miriam said quietly. "I'm not like David. He's different, even though we're brother and sister. People are all different. God made us all that way."

"It'd be a pretty sorry world if everybody were just like me," David smiled. "It's God's variety that makes life interesting."

Mingo had never been so "nonplused" in his entire life. Before, he always had known exactly what he wanted to do and did it. Now, however, he found himself disturbed by the idea of leaving these people, and could not tell why.

"You don't have to decide right away," David said reassuringly. "We'll talk about it."

"One thing I promise you," Mingo said suddenly, "I'll never be against you. I'll never go back to the City. But they'll send others, you know."

A silence filled the room for they all realized that what Mingo had said was true. There was no way that the City would give up on its search for Starr and, when they came, they would have no compunction about wiping out all of the Remnant.

"I wish we could go on like we are," Josh said, suddenly breaking the silence. "Just hunting and fishing and living with each other out here."

"That's what I'd like," Mingo said at once, smiling at the boy, "But I guess things don't stay the same, do they?"

"Some things do," Starr said quietly. When Mingo looked at her, she said, "Love doesn't change." She reached over and took David's hand and held it. "Everything else may go, but when you love someone, that's like the sun coming up, it'll always be in the East."

"I'm glad you think that, Starr," Mingo said quietly, "And I hope you always do."

It was two days later that the messenger came. He came early in the morning before anyone was up. David heard the horse's hooves and sat up in bed. "Someone's out there," he said. Getting out of bed, he picked up his sword and walked to the door. Opening it, he slipped outside into the darkness. The sky was beginning to clear and he could see the outline of a rider, wearing a cloak. The wind was cold and there was snow in the upper reaches of the mountains waiting to come down. Shivering, he drew the cloak he had thrown about his shoulders closer and said quietly, "Who is it? What do you want?"

The horse champed at his bit and stomped the ground. A voice announced, "I have a message from Goel."

Goel was the leader of the Christians in the City, a man whom David trusted implicitly. For one moment David suspected a trap and moved closer. "Who are you?" he asked.

Then he was surprised when the answer came. "Don't you know me, David? It's me, Will Sigma."

"Get down!" David cried at once. He heard a noise behind him and saw that Starr had come also. "It's Will Sigma," he said, "With a message from the City."

Will got down off his horse, tied him quickly, and the three went back into the house. David lit a candle and the tiny yellow flame threw its feeble illumination around the room. Will looked tired, his face edged tight with fatigue as he straightened his shoulders wearily. "It's been a long ride," he said. "Could I have something to drink?"

"Of course." Starr quickly went across the room and returned at once with a large goblet of water. Will drank thirstily and, when he handed the cup back, she said, "More?"

Will shook his head, "That's enough for now." He stretched and arched his back and made a grimace. "I'm getting to be an old man," he said wryly. "I can remember the time when a ride like that would have been just fun."

"It must be important," David said. "Is something going on?"

"Well, you might say that." Will hesitated, then grinned. "One thing's going on, I've become one of you."

"Will! You've become a Christian!" David exclaimed. He came at once and threw his arm around the smaller man's shoulders and gave him an enthusiastic hug. "That's wonderful! I'm so glad for you."

"So am I Will. Welcome into the family!" Starr said. She took his hand warmly and exclaimed, "The others will be so glad!"

"Well, it came as quite a shock to me," Will said. "I can't really believe that I've done it." He looked a little downcast and said, "I've made a few bad remarks about you folks, Christians in general. But now," he threw his shoulders back and smiled beautifully, "I've never been so happy in my life." Then the smile suddenly left his face and he shook his head, "But, I've got news for you. You've got to get out of here."

"Leave the Badlands?" David asked at once, his face troubled.

"No, not just the Badlands. You've got to get out of the Fields.

Goel says you are to come back to the City. He says that's what the Lord has told him."

The news came as a shock to both David and Starr. Starr asked, "Did he say why?"

"Well, Goel doesn't usually give many details, but I can guess." He sat down wearily in a chair at the single rough-hewn table and said, "Somehow word has come out that they're going to launch a terrible search of the Fields. Things have gone to pot in the City. The manuals have gone down, many of them, to the Shadowland to avoid the persecution of Christians. Richard Xi has declared war, in effect."

"He needs the manuals to keep things running." David said.

"That's true, and he needs the people out here to raise the grain to make the alcohol. Otherwise, we wouldn't have any fuel. But, he's decided to root out all the Christians and there's a reward out for anyone who'll turn a Christian in. Many Christians have been captured. Some have been executed."

"Why does he want us to come back? What good can we do there?"

"I can't say," Will replied. "His message is that he wants you and all your people back."

"Where will we go?" Starr asked quietly.

"The only safe place now is underneath the City, down in the Shadowland. There are so many passageways and hidden places down there that even the Peacekeepers are afraid to go. They get lost. They are also afraid that if they execute the wrong ones the whole City will blow up. All of the electrical components are there, the plumbing, everything is run from down there. So, they have to be careful." Will sighed and said, "It's not a very happy life, but if that's what Goel says. You'll be safer there."

"alright. We'll leave at once," David announced. "You'd better go to bed and rest while we get ready."

Starr saw to it that Will had a place to sleep and David went about the camp passing the word along to the other leaders. It took a while to gather their things together but, by late afternoon the wagons were filled, the animals hitched, and they left the camp.

Mingo walked alongside Miriam as they left. He looked back and said, "I'll never forget this place."

"Where are you going, Mingo?" Miriam asked. "We're all going back to the City. You said you'd never go back there."

"I can go part of the way, at least." The truth was, Mingo was not at all sure what to do. He felt free from any obligation to report back to Richard Xi or Leo Zeta. He had no loyalties to them whatsoever. His loyalties lay with these people, he suddenly realized, especially to this young woman beside him. He could not forget that she had nursed him back to health and shown him nothing but love when he had come to destroy her family.

He said little to her that day, but became one of the scouts. Along with Will, he knew the country better than anyone. The two of them moved ahead and twice in the next three days they saved the Remnant from destruction. The Peacekeepers were already out in full force and it took great skill to avoid them.

On the night before they would reach the river and cross into the City, they made camp in a barren spot sheltered only by a few stunted trees. There was a small creek of sorts, but that night they did not cook because they didn't want to be revealed by their campfires.

Mingo stood at the edge of the camp, his eyes searching the horizon. He heard a sound, and in one smooth motion drew his sword and stood on guard.

"It's only me." Josh had come out of the darkness to stand beside the man.

Sheathing the sword, Mingo said, "Pretty quiet in camp. I miss the singing."

"You always did like our hymns, didn't you?"

"Yes, I did." Mingo had a talent for music, a fine singing voice. He had listened to the hymns sung to God at the meetings and had memorized most of them. He would sing them under his breath until they became a part of him. He could not get away from the theme that God is all, He loves people, and gave His Son to die for them. Somehow this stayed with him, even more than the preaching. Perhaps this was because it was set to music.

"Are they having a service tonight?"

"No, David said we'll wait until we get into the City. Did you know there are Ecclesias all over the place? They have to hide, though, or the Peacekeepers will arrest them."

"So I understand. Are you afraid, Josh?"

"A little bit. But God will take care of us."

"You really believe that, don't you?"

"Why, sure, don't you?" Josh stopped abruptly, "You do believe in God don't you, Mingo? You never say anything, but I know you do."

Mingo had been thinking of God a great deal during his stay with the Remnant. He had said nothing to anyone, but the preaching, the hymns, and the lives of the simple people loving each other, had reached into him. Now, in the silence of the night he freely admitted, "Yes, I never thought of God much before, but since I've been with you and your people, Josh, He seems very real."

"Why don't you just love Him? That's all He wants, so far as I can figure out."

"That's a funny thing to say. I thought people were supposed to serve God."

"They are, but you always serve the ones you love, don't you? I mean, just look around. People who love each other take care of each other. It's not hard." This simple philosophy came from Josh without thought. It was part of his very life. He had learned it when he was a child, but it was a new thought to Mingo.

"I never thought of it like that," Mingo said. "Maybe because I never had any friends or family. I always had to look out for myself."

The silence ran on and finally Josh said abruptly, "I wish you'd become a Christian. Then you could marry Miriam and you would be my real brother."

Mingo started. He turned and looked at Josh and said, "Why, she'd never have a rough fellow like me."

"Yes, she would."

"What makes you say that?" Mingo asked curiously. "Did she say something to you?"

"I can tell," Josh said confidently. "I've been watching her a long time. All the young men come to court her cause she's so pretty, but she doesn't like any of them. She likes you. I can tell because she watches you when you don't know it. Her eyes are always on you."

Mingo was startled at the thought and he shook his head. "She'd never have a man who didn't believe like she does."

"That's right," Josh agreed. "But you already believe in God. That's more than you did when you came here." He reached out and touched the sleeve of the man, saying, "Some day you'll believe in Jesus, and when you do, I bet you'll be my *real* brother.

Chapter Fifteen

A Church In The Shadowland

"It's different here, isn't it?" Starr asked quietly. She was sitting beside David in a small cubicle of a room. It contained a bed made out of plastic, pipe tubing glued together and covered with leather thongs, and a mattress of sorts. The only other furniture was a battered chest that bulged with the belongings they had brought to the Shadowland.

David looked around the cheerless room and nodded, "It isn't much, but we're lucky to have a place to lie down."

He looked discouraged. Starr reached over and took his hand. The two sat on pads that served in place of chairs. "It's alright," she assured him. "We won't be here forever."

David shrugged his shoulders. "It's hard to say. Our people are arrested every day. Did you know that there was another execution yesterday?"

"I heard about it. Punch said that three of our own people were put to death. But, he said, they went out singing the praises of God."

David got to his feet and stretched nervously. "They're better off than we are, aren't they?"

It was unlike him to be so discouraged and Starr stood and put her arms around him. "As long as we're together, we can face anything. Isn't that right?"

"Yes, it is. Come along. It's almost time for the service."

They left the cubicle and joined others who were making their way down the gloomy, half-lit tunnel. Along the edge of the tunnel ran pipes that carried the water and sewage from the City. On the other side were sealed tubes that carried the wiring that fed electricity from the huge dynamo that created the power for Dome City. There were dimly-glowing lights every fifty feet and, as they moved along with the others, David said, "I was surprised when Mingo decided to come to the Shadowland with us."

"So was I," Starr agreed. "He loves the outdoors so much—he was in prison for a long time. Josh was glad that he decided to come. Those two are very close."

"Yes, they are." David looked up ahead and saw the people turning down another corridor. "That's where the Ecclesia will meet this time. A little strange to have a church service in a different place, but we have to to avoid the Peacekeepers. Watch your step! These pipes are tricky." Some of the pipes ran across the floor and Starr picked her way carefully.

When they turned down the corridor, Starr saw that it opened up into a large room filled with people. "There must be two-hundred here," she remarked. "I don't even know some of them."

"There's no place big enough to hold all of us." David said. "I suppose this way, we'll get to meet members of other Ecclesias to hear different preachers and teachers."

They made their way to the back of the crowd and David said to Starr, "You're not tall enough to see over this crowd. Let's go to the side."

"Alright. I like to see the preacher."

They made their way to the side where David found a place for her to stand so she could see clearly. Suddenly she said, "Look! There's Mingo over there with Josh and Miriam."

David looked across the room and saw the three. "Yes. Miriam tells me Mingo is getting close to giving his life to God."

"I think Mingo had two reasons for coming with us."

"Really? What are they?"

"You know. One is, he's hungry for God." Starr studied Mingo's face which was in repose. "He's never seen anything like Christians living together. He's just like I was when I first came to the Fields. I couldn't believe it when I saw love so free and unrestrained. I didn't know anything about things like that. And neither did Mingo."

"It's hard for him to take it all in. He's had a rough life," David agreed. "What's the other reason?"

Starr pinched his arm. "You know! Don't play dumb with me. He's in love with Miriam."

"You're the expert at falling in love," David grinned. "I'm just a poor dumb husband."

"Sometimes I think you are," Starr said with irritation. "Other times I think you're just plain dumb."

"I hope you never find out which one," David said. They had a playful way of speaking to one another, always had. And now, that they were married, they were more in love than ever.

"Look! There's the preacher. He's with Goel."

Goel, the leader of the Christians, was one of the outstanding preachers of the church that had spread itself over the entire City. This tall man with chiseled features, held up his hand for silence, saying, "Beloved, we are here together to worship the Lord. Now, lift your voices. Let God know how much we love Him."

As he said these words, Miriam was very conscious of Mingo, who was standing beside her. She began singing the songs—all simple praise songs giving glory to God. She was not surprised to hear Mingo also singing quietly. He had a beautiful voice. She had heard him sing other songs when he would lift his voice and let the power of it practically raise the roof. Now, however, he was almost speaking the words—"Jesus Christ, the Son of God, strong Son of God, we praise your Name . . ."

The singing went on for nearly an hour. Sometimes there would be a pause, then a spoken word of encouragement from one of the Elders. At other times there would be silence, except for the sound of people quietly praying to God. At other times, the sound would sweep through the whole room, filling it with the praise of God. Finally Goel said, "We will now listen while our brother brings the Word of Life to us. You know Brother Andrew. He is one of God's anointed men. Listen to what God has given him."

Brother Andrew was a short man, middle-aged with a short beard. His appearance was not at all impressive and it always came as a surprise when he opened his mouth and his tremendously powerful voice uttered the words of the sermon. He began by saying, "Of old, God has said one thing about the inhabitants of earth. After Adam and Eve fell, all men were alienated from God. That is why God has said, 'Ye must be born again'."

Mingo listened as the preacher spoke of the necessity of turning from self and sin to God. Since he had been with the Remnant he had often heard about being "born again." Somehow he was unable to take it in. When the preacher spoke of Nicodemus asking, "How can a man be born when he is old? Can he enter the second time into his mother's womb and be born?" Mingo somehow knew that it was true—yet he could not apply it to himself.

Josh was listening to the preacher, and at the same time keeping an eye on his friend, Mingo. *I wish he would just give up and quit trying to understand it,* Josh thought. *No one really understands it, but I know it works.*

Mingo turned toward Josh and saw the eagerness on his face. He looked away quickly thinking, *The boy wants me to be born again, whatever that means, but I don't know how.* He listened intently for the next hour as the preacher spoke lovingly, sometimes with great power, sometimes warning of the wrath to come. Over and over again the words "Ye must be born again," fell from his lips and always was followed by the warning, "Only in Jesus can a man find God."

The service reached its end and many went to the front of the room to be prayed for by the Elders of the Ecclesia. The sick were prayed for, also widows and orphans who were under the care of the Ecclesia. It was like nothing that Mingo had ever seen before. And, as he stood there, there was an urge in him to move forward, to join those who were kneeling. But he resisted it. Mingo was embarrassed, not knowing why. After the benediction, Josh said, "That was a great sermon, wasn't it, Mingo?"

Mingo nodded saying, "He's a great speaker, even though he looks ordinary."

Miriam said, "You can tell he has spent many hours with God. There's always that aura that rests over a man or woman who prays a great deal."

Mingo shot her a quick glance. "I think you're right, although I don't know much about these things."

The three joined the crowd that was leaving the room and, as they left, they did not notice a small man wearing nondescript clothing. There was no reason they should notice him for he had made himself deliberately unobtrusive.

The man turned and joined the crowd as they made their way to the elevators that ascended to the City above. He got off and soon was in front of the White Tower. Taking a deep breath, he entered and demanded to see Richard Xi. The guard looked at him scornfully. "He's not ready to see you. You'll have to write a letter asking for an audience."

The nondescript man reached into his pocket, pulled out a slip of paper and handed it to the guard. Reading it, the guard's face showed surprise and he shook his head. "I don't see why he'd want to see you, but go on in." He handed the slip of paper back and the man slipped in to the office of Richard Xi. He found Xi looking up at him over the desk.

"Well, have you got anything for me?"

"I think it's time to take them in," he said. "I've just come from one of their meetings. If your men had been there, they could have grabbed the leaders." Carefully the man removed his cloak, then went over to sit down in the chair across from Xi. He spoke as an equal. Since he was such a valuable spy arrogance had come into him. "It won't be too hard," he said. "The next meeting is in two days. Of this group anyway. There are over fifty groups."

"How long before we can get them all?"

"I don't think you have to get them all." The spy, whose name was Malthous, smiled confidently. "I know who the leaders are now and I know where they stay. Here's the list. If you take these, the rest will be like sheep without a leader."

Richard Xi took the list eagerly and looked over it. "You've done a good job Malthous. I'll take over from here. Your credits will be placed to your account as usual." He smiled, "What are you going to do with all that money?"

"Spend it on myself, what else?"

The raids came abruptly without warning. The leaders of the Ecclesias were apprehended by small groups of Peacekeepers. There was no time to run. They did not come in large groups so as not to give alarm. Instead of their white uniforms, they wore disguises. This was the plan of Saul Lambda and it worked to perfection.

David and Starr were taken first. They were wakened out of a sound sleep, grabbed by the iron-handed men whose eyes blazed with triumph. No less a man than Leo Zeta himself made the arrest. The fat man stood grinning at the pair and said, "Well, you've led me a merry chase, but it's all over now."

Starr felt the beginning of fear run along her nerves, but David put his arm around her. At once it seemed to fade away. David said, "We won't resist. Do with us what you have to."

"Exactly what I intend to do," Leo Zeta said. He turned to the guard and said, "Put the irons on them. If they try to escape, kill them. But, we want to keep them alive. I want to see them when they tell everyone that this Christ they love so much is nothing but a fraud."

David wanted to respond, but he saw the cruelty in the eyes of Zeta and knew that it would only give the man pleasure. He said, "We're ready."

"Take them away then!" Zeta snapped, disappointed at not having provoked a response.

As they were taken along, David saw others of the leaders being hustled along, chained hand and foot. The chains made an ominous clinking sound as they snapped the manacles on his own wrist and feet, and then followed suit on Starr. It took all his courage to smile and say, "We'll be alright, Starr. God will be with us."

The raid was over in twenty-four hours. Not everyone was taken from the Shadowland, of course. Richard Xi had made that plain. "Take only the leaders," he said. "Once they are gone, the others will be easy to handle. Someone has to take care of the work."

Starr and David were separated. Starr was placed with the women. She was glad to see that Miriam was not one that was taken.

By the same token, David, was glad that Josh was not one of the captives. He knew it was part of the scheme of their captors to keep him and Starr separated. For the next two days David was ruthlessly interrogated. Truth serum was shot into his veins and he told them exactly what he would have told them had it not been done—that he was a follower of Jesus Christ and meant no danger to the state. His chief concern was for Starr and the other leaders. He had reached the point where he knew it was out of his hands.

David, along with Starr and the other leaders, were brought before Richard Xi. Looking down at them from a platform to where they stood manacled Xi said, "This would be so easy if you would simply recant." He talked for some time about the rosy future that would lie before them if they would simply deny Jesus Christ. When he paused and said, "What is your answer?" it was Goel who spoke for all of them. "He has been faithful to us. How could we turn on the God who has never done us wrong?"

"Very well. So be it," Richard Xi said, his face reddening. "I expected nothing else. "You will be relieved. We cannot let your infection spread throughout the City. You've already done enough damage. Take them away!"

When they were all out of the room, Saul Lambda asked, "Richard, what do we do about the others? We have the leaders but the others are heretic, believing in this Christ of theirs."

"We'll have a reclamation program for them. It's time to try what our scientists have come up with."

"What they used to call a 'lobotomy'?" Lambda raised his eyebrows. "It hasn't worked too well in the past. It'll turn them into nothing but machines."

"So be it!" Xi snapped. "As long as we've found the way to mitigate the effects so that they'll be able to do their work. They won't know much of anything, but they've brought it on themselves. They're insane anyway. They'll be better off without their fantasies."

"When will all this start?"

"The program will start after the execution. We'll take them a few at the time so that the work can be done. We'll put them back in line again after we've cured them of their infection."

Inside his cell, David talked with the other men for a time. They prayed and finally, David said, "I don't see any hope, Goel."

Goel looked up. His head had been bowed and his eyes were calm as was his voice. "There have been other men of God and women too in prisons throughout the ages. It may be that we will die in this place, but if we die, we die trusting God."

Something about his simple statement seemed to cheer the others and they began to pray again. It was a small cell, but somehow it was not lonely. The men felt the Spirit of the Lord passing from one to the other and instead of fear and doubt there was a note of joy as they began to sing praises to God.

Chapter Sixteen

A New Way For Mingo

Mingo was awakened out of a deep sleep by the sound of voices. He is like those who do not awaken gradually, but seem to snap from a deep sleep into full consciousness. He lay there on the hard pad wondering what was happening, then stood to his feet with a smooth fluid motion. Quickly he slipped into his tunic, stepped into his sandals, then moved across the floor, careful to avoid the sleeping forms of those with whom he shared the room. Some began to stir but none awakened.

Mingo slipped through the door and glanced down the long gloomy corridor. He saw moving figures and the sounds of the voices came in with clarity.

"Alright, get along there. You can't get away."

Mingo stepped back into the shadows. The bulky shapes of twisted pipes and curving conduits were everywhere. He found them to be a convenient place to stand and watch. His senses were alert, much as if he were hunting in the woods. Soon he saw a procession coming down the tunnel. He grew apprehensive when he saw one of his new friends, Zacharias, a member of the Ecclesia, who sometimes taught. Zacharias was chained to another man that Mingo did not recognize. On each side of them strolled a burly Peacekeeper. They wore white uniforms and carried weapons loosely in one hand. The other hand held the arms of the captives.

Mingo watched them pass, then he saw that others were coming. It was a group of more than ten, including women and children. A sudden thought came to him. *It's a raid! I've got to get Miriam and Josh out of here!*

After the small group passed, Mingo dodged out from the covert of the pipes, then ran in the opposite direction from the captives. He made several turns before he arrived at a doorway. He hurriedly knocked on the door. Almost at once he heard the sound of someone inside. "Who is it?" someone asked.

"It's me Josh, open the door!"

Josh pulled the door back and Mingo said quickly, "Come on! We've got to get away! They're arresting all the Christians, some of them anyway."

Josh rubbed his eyes and asked, "Where are we going?"

"Down deeper than they'll care to follow. Come on, let's get Miriam!"

The two made their way to the women's quarters. Mingo gave the alarm and Miriam came at once. An older woman said, "They may not arrest all of us."

Miriam said, "I'm not taking any chances. I'm going with Mingo. Come on Josh."

The three of them left and Mingo, who had done a great deal of exploring during his short stay, led them down a twisting labyrinthine way. They passed numerous doorways, massive machinery and soon began to hear a mighty hum as of millions of bees.

"What's that?" Josh demanded in alarm.

"It's the dynamo. Runs all the electrical part of the City."

There was something frightening about the power of the huge machine they approached. It occupied what would be several city blocks. Their ears rang from the overpowering humming noise.

"Let's get out of here," Mingo said quickly. "I can't take this.

I don't think the Peacekeepers can either. As far as I know, they don't come down here either."

He led them past the dynamo where some of the Shadow-men who were on duty gave them a curious look. None of them spoke and soon the sound of the dynamo grew faint as Mingo led them deeper and deeper down several ladders.

"What's down here, Mingo?" Miriam asked.

"I'm not sure. Some of the machinery. Not very pleasant, but we'll be safe here until we find out what's going on."

Eventually they reached the end of their quest. The stairs came to an end and there were several corridors that led off. They discovered it was storage for tools and spare parts for the equipment that kept the City running. They found a room with a little furniture in it, a small electric cook stove and a cabinet full of food.

"Looks like the workers might use this," Mingo said. "I don't think they'll come this far."

There were several chairs in there and all three of them sat down. Miriam's face was pale. The single small bulb barely lit the place. It was like living way down deep in the ocean with light coming from far above. It gave a gargoyle impression that frightened Miriam.

"How long will we have to stay here, Mingo?"

"I don't know. If I had my way, we'd get out of here right now. Get back to the Fields."

"I'd like that too," Josh said quickly, "But we can't leave until we get everyone together."

"We can't leave until the Elders say so," Miriam reminded him.

They sat there quietly, speaking from time-to-time until, Mingo grew restless. "I'll go see what I can find out. You two should be alright here. From the looks of this place, no one's been here in a long time. See if you can take some of that food and make it edible. I'll be back as soon as I can."

"Don't leave us, Mingo." Miriam moved over to stand beside him and put her hand on his chest. Her lips trembled—she looked very vulnerable. "I'm afraid to stay here."

Josh stood also. "Can't we go with you?"

Mingo looked down at the two and felt a sense of responsibility. "Look," he said, "I won't be gone long, I promise. I'll go back and talk to some of the Elders. At least find out what's going on. What I think," he said slowly, "Is that Richard Xi and his thugs are trying to pin down all the Christians."

His answer sobered them, although they half-expected it. Unconsciously, Mingo reached down, took the hands of the two and smiled. He looked strong and totally dependable as he stood there. "I wouldn't leave you if I thought there was any danger. But, we've got to know what's going on. I won't leave unless you agree."

Miriam reached over and put her arm around Josh. "We'd just be a handicap, Josh." She looked at the man in front of her then said in almost a whisper, "You go ahead, Mingo. I know you'll take care of us."

Mingo was struck by her remark. He nodded, then hurriedly left. As he made his way back to the surface, Miriam's words kept echoing in his head, *I know you'll take care of us.*

Mingo could not get away from them. He had never made it his business to take care of anyone, but now, he somehow wanted to. As he wound his way around, avoiding the Peacekeepers that appeared from time-to-time, he said to himself, "I never had to take care of anyone—never wanted to, but now—it feels *right.*

A small group of the Elders who had escaped had found a secret compartment. They had been led there by one of the Shadow-men who had lived his life underground. He knew nothing about life in the Dome City, certainly not about the Fields, but he knew every inch of the Shadowland. Mingo had met him once and, when he had spoken with the man, whose name was Ebon, he discovered what had happened. "Take me to the Elders," he said.

"I don't know," Ebon said nervously. "You're not one of us, are you?"

Mingo hesitated. It would be easy to lie but he chose to be honest. "No, I'm not a Christian, but I want to help. Look, at least go tell them I want to see them. I've got David's sister and brother hidden away. They need to know what's happening."

Ebon agreed to that. "You wait here," he ordered. "I'll be back."

He left and returned within twenty minutes and then led Mingo to a small apartment where seven of the Elders were gathered. Mingo had heard one of them speak; it was Caleb, a tall man with white hair. At once Mingo said, "I know you don't have any reason to trust me. But I'm trying to take care of David's sister and brother. I assume it's a raid to get all of the Christians."

"That is right, my son," Caleb said calmly. "Many have been captured and taken, especially among the leaders. Only those of us here are left."

"What's going to happen?" Mingo demanded. "Are you going to stay or try to make it to the Fields?"

"The Lord has told us to stay where we are, that He will deliver us," Caleb said. He looked around the circle with a troubled glance. "At the moment, we do not know *how* that will happen."

"What can I do with Miriam and Josh? I'll take care of them, and anyone else, as well as I can. I'm not one of you," he admitted, "But I'm *for* you."

The Elders looked at each other and Caleb smiled, "You're not far from the Kingdom, my son."

Mingo paused unaware of the meaning. He saw the Elders looking at him strangely and suddenly it came to him, *They want me to join them.*

As if he had read Mingo's thought, Caleb said, "I've talked with David about you. He feels that God is calling you away from your life into a new life with Him. May I talk with you about it?"

"But I have to get back—"

"It will not take long," Caleb suggested. "It might make the difference—all the difference in the world to you."

"Well, I suppose I have a little time."

Mingo never forgot what occurred in the next thirty minutes. It was so simple he could not believe it. Caleb was a man of infinite kindness, he discovered, and Mingo, who had his guard up with most people, found himself totally at ease with the older man. The two of them went to a very small room, sat down, and Caleb opened a worn Bible. He began to read from it, almost casually quoting Scripture-after-Scripture. They all tied together somehow and Mingo found, for the first time, that Christianity was making sense to him.

"This world we live in is enemy-occupied territory. It's not the world as God first made it," Caleb said in a kindly fashion. "When man *fell*, everything *fell*, even nature. But one day, there'll be a new world. All evil will be out of it and confined to a single place. We, all those who love God and serve His Christ, will not be troubled with pain, sickness, or death."

A longing began to grow in Mingo that he could not explain. He felt an utter dissatisfaction with his old life—the disgust that had often risen with it and said, "God wouldn't want me. You don't know the things I've done."

"All men are sinners. We haven't all sinned alike, but we've all sinned. We all come to God as wounded, bruised, disobedient children, and God welcomes us. He puts His arms around us the minute we turn to Him."

"Like that prodigal son that I heard the preacher talk about!" Mingo exclaimed.

"Exactly like that," Caleb nodded enthusiastically. He went on reading Scripture, then said, "Do you believe in God, Mingo?"

"Yes, I do."

"You've heard much about Jesus. You've seen how He has transformed the lives of many."

"Yes, I have. I know that He's real."

"Then, one thing remains. Will you ask Him to save you, to come into your life?"

"But, I don't see Him."

"Christ is everywhere. Like the Father, He is in all places, He is in all times. All we need to do as sinners is call on Him. Will you do that?"

Mingo felt that he was on a tightwire above a precarious gulf. He felt that if he had made one single mistake at this point he would forever be a lost man. Somehow he knew that all of his life had led up to this one moment, this one moment in this tiny room, listening to this one man. The words of the Scripture seemed to hang in the air. *Repent—Believe—Call upon Me!*

It was almost as if they were an echo inside his head and chest. He began to perspire and his hands trembled. He was afraid and did not know why. Most of all he was afraid of making an awful, eternal mistake.

Caleb leaned forward and saw the distress in the young man's spirit. "I know what you're going through. Many of us go through that. You're afraid to turn, afraid to go on and can't go back."

"That's it," Mingo gasped. "That's what I feel like."

"Then you must choose. Either go back and be what you were—or call upon Jesus Christ to save you from what you are and put His life into you. Call upon Him, Mingo! He's never failed one time to hear a sinner's cry."

Mingo sat there trembling and then, in a voice hoarse with

desperation said, "Oh, Christ, save me from what I am. Make me to be what *You* want me to be!"

The two men were alone, and yet, as Mingo cried out to God, it seemed the room was filled with the presence of God. Nothing could be seen, nothing changed to the eyes, but Mingo knew that he was not alone!

Then, Mingo looked up; his eyes filled with tears. "Something's happened to me," he whispered. "All the anger and all the doubt is gone."

"Christ has come into your heart. That's what He does."

"Will it always be like this?" Mingo asked.

"He will always be there, but there may be times when you'll be troubled and feel alone. That's when you have to believe and trust that He's there, even when you don't feel Him."

"What do we do now?"

"You have been *converted—born again.* You are now a Christian. You will remember this day for the rest of your life, my son. You will spend your life *being* the Christian that you have just *become*."

"I don't know anything," Mingo said almost frantically.

"That is what Elders are for. That is what friends are for. Your brothers and sisters in the Ecclesia—they will help you. Now you are like a baby in your spirit. But you will grow fast as you study the Word, learn to pray, and be obedient to the commands of Christ."

For some time Caleb consoled Mingo. Then he said, "Come, we must tell the others that we have a new brother in the Lord."

As soon as Mingo entered the small room, Josh and Miriam stood to their feet.

"What did you find out?" Miriam asked nervously. "Is David alright, and Starr?"

"They've been taken captive, along with most of the leaders." Mingo gave them the bad news and then began to explain all that he had learned.

"Then it's hopeless," Miriam said.

Mingo hesitated, then shook his head. "I don't think so. What have I heard you say? God will take care of us."

Miriam was stunned. She looked up into Mingo's face and something kept her silent. Josh was studying Mingo's face, too. Smiling, Mingo said, "I've got something to tell you!"

"I know what it is. There's something different about you! You've become a Christian!" Miriam whispered.

Mingo dropped his head and stared at the floor. He was still filled with the joy that had come to him. When he looked up there were tears in his eyes. He had never cried since he was a child, but now, tears ran down his cheeks as he nodded mutely.

I'm so glad for you, Mingo," she whispered. "So very glad."

Finally, Miriam pulled back and dabbed at her eyes with a handkerchief, "I'm so glad for you, Mingo," she whispered. "So very glad."

"Me, too," Josh said. "Now we're really brothers, aren't we?"

"Yes, that's what the Elders said, that everybody in the Ecclesia were my brothers and my sisters." He wiped his face and tried to smile. "I've never had anyone. Now, I've got a big family."

The three could not seem to talk fast enough about what had happened. They were eager for Mingo to relate every detail.

Then in desperation he said, "That's all I can remember."

"You men are all alike," Miriam said. "You just tell the headlines. Women want to know the fine print."

"Well, I—it might take a long time. And, I'm not sure I understand it all myself. All I know is, I'm going to do whatever Jesus says, no matter what it costs."

When they had calmed down, Miriam asked, "Did the Elders give you any duty?"

Mingo looked at her strangely, "How did you know that?"

"I didn't know it."

"You were right. The Elders said they needed me. Caleb said they needed a man who could get around to try to find some way to help those who are still out there avoiding capture."

"What about those who are already captured?" Josh demanded. "What about David and Starr?"

"I've been thinking about that. Somehow we've got to get them out of that prison."

"That's impossible!" Miriam said, then caught herself. "But nothing's impossible with God."

"I hope not, because I'm going to try. But I've got to have help."

"I'll help!" Josh said at once.

"Sure you will." Mingo threw his arms around the boys shoulders and looked at Miriam. "One thing has been coming into my mind. I know I'm not smart enough to think of it, so maybe the Lord put it there."

"What is it, Mingo?"

"Will Sigma and Michael Kappa—they know all the Border Guards. They've told me over and over again the Border Guards are about ready for a revolt."

"That's right," Miriam agreed instantly. "Will told me that most of them hate the City. They hate what goes on but they have to stay because their families are captives. They are held hostage."

"I'm going to find those two and the three of us are going to somehow pull the plug on this thing."

"What about us?" Miriam asked quickly.

"I want you to come with me. I wouldn't feel safe leaving you here."

A warm glow spread through Miriam and she dropped her eyes. "I'm glad you feel that way, Mingo."

Josh watched the two and blurted out, "Why don't you two just get married!"

"Josh!" Miriam exclaimed, her face flushing.

But Mingo smiled, "I was going to get around to that. I have been watching some of the young people in the group, trying to learn about romance and how to court a young lady. That was my plan to come around and bring presents and write poems; the things you're supposed to do. But, I guess I might as well warn you that I'm joining the bunch that's following you around—the bunch of suitors trying to get you to marry them."

"They don't matter," Miriam said quietly. Then she lifted her eyes and smiled, "But you do. I've always known it."

Ignoring Josh, Mingo reached out and put his arms around her. She came to him. "I don't have anything to offer and I'll probably make a million mistakes, but I love you." He paused and said in a voice of wonder, "That's the first time I ever said 'I love you' to anyone, the first time in my whole life."

"I love you, too, Mingo, and yes, I'll marry you. But, when we get out of this, I'll expect a little more courting. A girl has that much coming."

Josh watched as the two held each other and when they looked down at him and smiled, he said, "I'm glad that's settled. Now, how're we going to get David and Starr out of this mess they're in?"

Chapter Seventeen

A Matter Of Love

Richard Xi sat at his desk, a smile on his thin lips. He did not smile often, and when he did it usually was a sign of misfortune for those who sat under his authority. However, smile was somewhat broader than usual.

Picking up a pen, he leaned back in his chair and stared at the blank wall opposite him. It was a matter of his pride that no pictures, trophies, or anything of a personal nature be displayed in his office. He was totally dedicated to bringing enlightenment to those who did not succumb to the tenets of the City.

A small light blinked over the door and Xi commanded, "Enter!"

The door hissed open noiselessly and Saul Lambda entered followed by Leo Zeta. Both men had self-satisfied looks on their faces and, as they came to stand before Richard Xi's desk, Lambda said, "Mission accomplished."

"You've done a good job," Xi responded, nodding firmly. It was rare praise indeed, for he did not believe in handing out bouquets very often. Now, however, he was satisfied and said so. "It's been a hard chase and we've suffered many setbacks. But, as enemies of the City, these Crossbearers will now pay the penalty for being out of step with the truth."

"They'll pay the penalty, alright," Leo Zeta grunted. The

smile on his thick lips broadened, "Practically everyone in the City will be there to watch the execution."

"Please, not execution. The 'relieving'," Xi protested. "The people must learn to look on this in a scientific manner. When anyone in the state has opinions that differ from the truth, they must be eliminated. It's like a growth in the body that's bringing disaster. It must be cut out."

Leo slapped his meaty hands together. "Well, they'll be cut out alright. I just wish we could give a little more dramatic illustration."

"What do you mean *more dramatic*?" Xi inquired.

"I mean, go back to some of the old forms of 'relieving'. I've been studying history. Back in the old days they had ways of relieving people that stuck in the mind. For instance, the hangman or the guillotine. When those heads 'popped off', that made an impression."

"You don't like our modern method of easing people out of the world?" Saul Lambda asked.

"No, it's just like going to sleep. They need to go out kicking and screaming, lots of blood, fear and terror."

"You're not far from being a primitive yourself, Leo," Richard Xi complained. "But you'll see that I'm right. Once we get rid of Starr Omega and that boyfriend of hers, along with their leaders and their little 'Ecclesia', things will be running again. Now, what I want . . ."

The words of Xi were cut off abruptly when the room was suddenly plunged into total darkness.

"What's going on?" Xi shouted. He groped for the console on his desk, found the switch that connected him to the Central Office, then punched it forcefully. Ordinarily a voice would speak; but now there was nothing.

Xi began shouting, "Guard! Guard!" as he stood to his feet. Stumbling across the room he collided with Lambda and the two of them did a comic dance trying to keep their balance. "Get out of my way!" Xi shouted.

"What's going on?" Leo said hoarsely.

"I don't know. Something's happened to the power but this time the emergency power's off, too," Xi said, a trace of fear threading his voice.

He groped his way to the door and pushed the emergency switch. When It did not move fear enveloped Xi. "We've got to get out of here!" he said. "Let me get a light!" He groped across the room, back to his desk, fumbled through a drawer on the right side and came up with a small battery pen light. It cast a slender beam across the room where he saw the faces of his two companions both filled with alarm.

"Something's gone wrong," Xi said, trying to keep his voice under control. "Come, we'll get to the bottom of this."

The three men moved out of the office. Zeta and Lambda staying close behind Xi. As they stepped into the outer office there was no difference. It too was cloaked in blackness. The clerk was scrambling through his desk trying to find a light. When he picked it up and turned it on, nothing happened. "Batteries are dead," he whispered. "What's going on, Sir?"

"I don't know. Go to emergency conditions."

The clerk began fumbling at a large console on his desk. He looked up and his eyes were wide with fright. "It's dead! What's happening? Why is all the power gone?"

"Come along, we'll go to Engineering. There's bound to be a simple explanation."

The three moved out of the office and made their way down a corridor. There was something eerie about the darkened corridors. Men and women were groping about. Screams were coming from all over the building. "The City's being destroyed!" a woman screamed, and at once the cry was taken up.

"The fools!" Xi shouted. "Go back to your desks. It'll be alright!"

He might as well have shouted to the tide, for there was a stampede. "We've got to get out of here!" Lambda said. "They'll stomp us to death."

Somehow they made their way down two flights of stairs until they came to the office marked Engineering. The automatic door was jammed. They could hear people on the other side crying, "Let me out! Let us out!"

Lambda remembered, "There's a manual release here. Let me see if I can do it." He fumbled in his pocket and came up with a small penknife and thrust it into a slight crevice. The door made a click and the three men managed to slide it back. Inside they were almost trampled by men who were fleeing the office. Xi staggered backwards and began shouting, "Don't leave! We've got to find out what's wrong!" Fear was rampant and soon the office was cleared.

Only three men remained inside, the Chief Engineer and his two assistants. Their faces were bleeding where they had fought with the mob. When they saw Richard Xi, the Engineer gasped, "What's going on?"

"You're the Engineer!" Xi snapped. "Why is there no power?"

"I can't say, Sir. Let me get an emergency light." He fumbled in a cabinet and came out with an old fashioned flashlight. At once he moved into the inner room. The other men followed him. Xi once again was intimidated by the banks of dials, levers and buttons. He had never understood how anyone could comprehend all of this. This was the brain-center of the entire City. Every command, every light switch, every bit of motivational power in the sleds, every elevator, all were controlled from this massive room.

The Engineer's hands flew like lightening over a large panel. He turned and shook his head. "The main system is down!"

"What does that mean?" Xi demanded.

"It means that the generator has been shut off. Until we get power from that generator, we're a dead City."

Another engineer said, "And, we're dead men, too. There's not much oxygen left. Besides, the people are going to panic and trample each other to death."

"They'll break out into the Fields," the third assistant said. "And, I'm going with them!"

"Stop!" the Engineer cried out. "Come back, you fool!" But his assistant was gone.

Xi said, "What's wrong with the generator?"

"Nothing, technically. Someone has intercepted the power. They've cut it off to this command post."

"I always told you that that was the weak link in our security, Xi," Saul Lambda grunted. He turned to Leo Zeta and said, "Get everyone as well-armed as you can. We've got to get down to that generator."

"It'll take some time to get some lights," Zeta said. He grabbed the flashlight from the engineer's hand and left the room calling, "I'll find out where the power's blocked."

Mingo moved down the darkened corridor as cautiously as a cat. He was not completely surprised that the staff had fled. He knew something about the fear that comes when darkness falls. He had seen it in the woods at night. Men who were brave as lions in the woods when the sun was out, were jumpy as field mice in the darkness of the night. So it had been in the Tower. Mingo had left the signal with Punch and the others to cut the power to the generator. "Be sure you give me time to get to the White Tower," he said. "As soon as you cut that switch there's going to be pandemonium. That's when I'll get the prisoners out."

As he moved along, he saw two guards, both holding flashlights before a door. "They didn't run away," he said. "They must be pretty good men."

As he approached, one of them said, "Any word from the generator? The air's getting pretty bad in here."

"They're working on it but one of you better go get some oxygen tanks. You're going to need them."

"Not me," the guard said. "I'm getting out of here. Are you coming?" he asked his fellow.

"No, someone's got to guard these prisoners."

"Be a fool and die then," the other guard snapped. He disappeared, running down the hallway.

Mingo moved closer and said, "What about the prisoners? There's not much air in there, is there?"

"Who cares? They're going to die anyway. If I had . . ."

He said no more—Mingo had struck him right between the eyes. He had been careful to put a small bar of iron in his fist so that the blow dropped the guard in a loose relaxed form on the floor.

Shooting the bolt, Mingo stepped over the body and, as the door flew open, he swung the light inside. "Come on, we're getting out of here." Suddenly he was met by David. Mingo grinned at him saying, "Time for the bridegroom to go meet the bride," he said. "Where do they keep the women?"

"Right down the hall," David said. "What's happened, Mingo?"

"We blew the generator. It'll take them some time to fix it. In the meanwhile, we've got to get out of here."

David turned and asked Goel, "What shall we do?"

"It's time to find a different place to hide. We will go to the Fields."

"I think that's sensible," David nodded. "Come, let's get the women and children out."

They moved down the hall, following Mingo who held the

light. One guard was on duty and when he saw the mob coming, he held his weapon high.

Mingo said, "I think you're outgunned, fellow." When the man hesitated, he reached out, took the weapon and said, "If I were you, I'd get out of here." He was taken at his word for the guard turned and fled down the hall.

David opened the door and called out, "Starr? You here?"

"Yes." At once Starr was in his arms and there was the happy sound of greetings as other men found their wives.

Mingo announced, "We'd better get out of here. We've got a little time, but sooner or later they'll get the generator going. Then, they'll be out for revenge."

David said, "Come on. Let's head for the Fields."

◆   ◆   ◆

Richard Xi stared in dismay at the report Saul Lambda had thrown down on his desk. There was a feeble light on. He had to strain his eyes. The generator had been restarted but had been so thoroughly sabotaged that only a fragment's of its power was available. Xi looked at the paper and asked, "This is all that's left?"

"That's all," Lambda growled. "They've all fled to the Fields. We've had to put the Peacekeepers to doing the manual work. Just barely able to keep the City going."

Leo Zeta said, "We've got a ghost town here, Xi. All we've got to do is go out in the Fields and capture some slaves to do the work."

"If you do that," Lambda snapped, "The whole thing will collapse. We're just barely keeping it going as it is."

Richard Xi's face was pale. He knew that both men who stood before him were hungry for power. As he looked at them he wondered how long it would be before one of them eliminated him in order to have his place. "Got to show authority," he said. He straightened up and said, "We'll get back our own." He voice sounded thin and feeble and he tried to make it stronger. "We've got the power, strength and truth. They're nothing but animals. This Jesus of theirs is nothing."

His voice trailed off into silence and somehow all three men knew that the City, as they had known it, would never be the same. The power of the White Tower was broken and those who had been slaves were now free.

◆   ◆   ◆

Mingo and Miriam walked alone beside the river. They had been silent for a long time; then Miriam said, "Has there come any word from the City? Are they coming after us?"

Mingo shrugged, "Maybe someday. Richard Xi died. We found that out—of natural causes." His eyes narrowed, "I would think Saul Lambda or Leo Zeta might be those 'natural causes,' but I don't think we have anything to fear, not for a while."

The air was cold. There was a sharpness and crispness in it and as the two walked along. Miriam was full of joy. She reached over and took the hand of Mingo. He stopped and looked at her in surprise. "What is it?" he asked.

"Nothing," she smiled. She looked fresh and very much alive as she stood there, the wind blowing her hair. "I'm just happy."

"So am I. I never thought I would be," Mingo said. "I am still amazed at how my life has changed. I wake up each morning filled with anticipation and joy that never leaves. It's so different, isn't it? I spent all my life trying to satisfy myself and got nothing. Once I gave up my life, I got everything."

"Everything?" Miriam whispered.

Mingo smiled at her and took her in his arms. "I've got the Lord—and I've got you—and somewhere down the line, we'll have children—a real family. What else is there?"

Miriam reached up and pulled his head down. "Nothing," she whispered. "That's all there is."

Mingo held her and the two clung to each other. Overhead the skies were dotted with white clouds that moved softly as the winds caressed them. The creek murmured in its bed and the memories that had haunted the two seemed to flee away. The future lay ahead. There might be dangers but, as Mingo held her he knew that all would be well. Slowly he released her and said, "Come along. I'll tell you how it's going to be."

"Alright." Miriam took his hand and the two moved slowly along the trail thinking of the days that were to come.

Books by Starburst Publishers

(Partial listing—full list available on request)

Beyond The River —Gilbert Morris & Bobby Funderburk

Book 1 in The Far Fields series is a a futuristic novel that carries the New Age and "politically correct" doctrines of America to their logical and alarming conclusions. In the mode of *Brave New World* and *1984*, *Beyond The River* presents a world where government has replaced the family and morality has become an unknown concept.

(trade paper) ISBN 0914984519 **$8.95**

God's Vitamin "C" for the Spirit —Kathy Collard Miller

Subtitled: *"Tug-at the-Heart" Stories to Fortify and Enrich Your Life.* Includes inspiring stories and anecdotes that emphasize Christian ideals and values by Barbara Johnson, Billy Graham, Nancy L. Dorner, Dave Dravecky, Patsy Clairmont, Charles Swindoll, H. Norman Wright, Adell Harvey, Max Lucado, James Dobson, Jack Hayford and many other well-known Christian speakers and writers. Topics include: Love, Family Life, Faith and Trust, Prayer, Marriage, Relationships, Grief, Spiritual Life, Perseverance, Christian Living, and God's Guidance.

(trade paper) ISBN 0914984837 **$12.95**

God's Vitamin "C" for the Spirit of WOMEN —Kathy Collard Miller

Subtitled: *"Tug-at-the Heart" Stories to Inspire and Delight Your Spirit."* A beautiful treasury of timeless stories, quotes and poetry designed by and for women. Well-known Christian women like Liz Curtis Higgs, Patsy Clairmont, Naomi Rhode and Barbara Johnson share from their hearts on subjects like Marriage, Motherhood, Christian Living, Faith and Friendship.

(trade paper) ISBN 0914984934 **$12.95**

A Woman's Guide To Spiritual Power —Nancy L. Dorner

Subtitled: *Through Scriptural Prayer.* Do your prayers seem to go "against a brick wall?" Does God sometimes seem far away or non-existent? If your answer is "Yes," you are not alone. Prayer must be the cornerstone of your relationship to God. "This book is a powerful tool for anyone who is serious about prayer and discipleship."

—Florence Littauer

(trade paper) ISBN 0914984470 **$9.95**

Purchasing Information:

Books are available from your favorite Bookstore, either from current stock or special order. To assist bookstore in locating your selection be sure to give title, author, and ISBN #. If unable to purchase from the bookstore you may order direct from STARBURST PUBLISHERS. When ordering enclose full payment plus $3.00 for shipping and handling ($4.00 if Canada or Overseas). Payment in US Funds only. Please allow two to three weeks minimum (longer overseas) for delivery. Make checks payable to and mail to STARBURST PUBLISHERS, P.O. Box 4123, LANCASTER, PA 17604. Credit card orders may also be placed by calling 1-800-441-1456 (credit card orders only), Mon-Fri, 8:30 a.m. – 5:30 p.m. Eastern Time. **Prices subject to change without notice.** Catalog available for a 9 x 12 self-addressed envelope with 4 first-class stamps. 8-97